A FATAL JOURNEY

BLYTHE BAKER

~

Perils and plots in British India...

When Rose Beckingham's pursuit of an international spy leads to the uncovering of an assassination plot, she'll have to race against time to prevent a crime before it occurs. The dangerous investigation will threaten her relationship with Achilles Prideaux, while leading her from the dusty streets of Morocco to the deep jungles of India.

With the roots of the mystery leading back to the deaths of the *real* Rose and her parents, the case is personal. Rose is drawn to the site of last summer's explosion, where a ruthless murderer strikes again. Can she discover the terrible secrets behind the fate of the Beckinghams before it's too late? Or will a mercenary killer escape and carry the truth away with him?

~

1

The air felt dusty on my skin, and the sun beat down relentlessly from above. It had been hot even before I'd taken chase, but now that I was physically exerting myself, I poured sweat. I knew powdery makeup would be running down my cheek, exposing the scar I worked so diligently to disguise, but I couldn't worry about that then. Not when I could see the shape of my target darting between stalls in the marketplace, trying to outrun me.

"Excuse me, Miss? Persimmons?" A woman, taking no notice of my rush, stepped in front of me, holding out a small orange fruit. Her accent was thick, and I knew she was a local.

I'd selected the wrong gown for a trip to the market. I had on a fine silk dress better suited for evening and cooler temperatures, and anyone with a keen eye for European fashions knew it marked me as wealthy. I couldn't take two steps without being offered something from someone. As it was, I had no time to politely decline or smile. I sidestepped the woman and carried on at a healthy pace, the breeze between the white-washed buildings on either side blowing my short blonde curls back.

Achilles had told me to never draw attention to myself. Discretion was a key part of our job, and sprinting through the city's largest marketplace was far from being discrete. However, I had long ago given up earning any praise from Achilles.

I paused in an archway, stretching onto the tips of my toes to try and find my target. Then, I saw his dark head and tan robes bob up and then dip below the crowd, like a coy fish in a pond. I took off after him once again, more determined than ever.

People crowded around stalls of fresh meats and vegetables, blocking a clear path. If I allowed my eyes to wander from the man for even a minute, he could be gone. My thin slippers did little to protect my feet from the rocks in the road. Dust kicked up over my legs, coating my stockings and the hem of my dress, but a little dust hardly mattered. People were already turning to stare as I ran past, bumping into crates of produce and nearly pushing over women whose arms were weighed down with their purchases. Shoppers shouted as I rushed past, telling me to slow down in Arabic, Spanish, French, and English. There wasn't a people group left whose ire I hadn't caught.

Thinking of ire made me remember Achilles Prideaux's face as I'd left him in the hotel's courtyard to give chase to the man who had just jumped from our employer's window, the same man I was chasing now. If I returned without any useful information, Achilles would be even more upset. It seemed I always earned the anger of my French companion one way or another. I did not have his patience, as proven by the foot chase I was currently involved in, and Achilles had more than once described me as impulsive. He explored every possibility before making a decision, whereas I chose the nearest path and ran headlong, stopping only once I'd hit a roadblock.

Thinking of a roadblock, I noticed the man's bobbing head suddenly stop, and it wasn't long before I saw the reason. As I closed the gap between us, I could see he was stalled at the corner of a street, wagons pulled by horses crossing in front of him like a river. He glanced over his shoulder, and I saw the pale tone of his skin. Though he wore traditional local garb, I did not suspect he was native to the area. As far as I knew, the man did not know me, but he understood I was following him, and he looked uncomfortable at how much distance I had gained.

I had no plan in place for what I'd do when I caught up to him. He didn't look to be a terribly large man, but it seemed safe to assume he could overpower me in a physical altercation. Was there a chance of a conversation? Could I convince him to release information to me willingly? Perhaps, but it seemed unlikely. The best I could hope for was to see his face closely and recognize him from among the many foreign friends we had made during our time investigating in the city or at least find out where in the city he was staying. Any scrap of information could help.

A vendor cut me off, a man with bundles of fabrics folded over his arm. He said something in Arabic, and I shook my head, trying to move past him. He matched my steps and moved on to what was probably the same speech in French.

"Please, sir," I said, gesturing for him to move. I leaned around the man's large frame and wares and could see my target shifting from foot to foot at the end of the road, just a few stalls away from me. The road was still too busy to cross, but it could clear any moment. Any delay could be the difference between success and failure.

The two desperate words were enough to let the man know I spoke English. "Nice fabrics. Good Price. You like?"

Frustrated, I ducked under his arm and jumped over a wooden crate of apples. People gasped and moved out of my way, looking at me like I might be crazy, and in that moment, I was half-crazed. I had one aim. With my path to the end of the road now clear, I realized I could no longer see the man. He'd disappeared.

I spun on the spot, searching to see where he could have gone. I looked back down the way I'd just come to see if he had somehow slipped past me while I'd been distracted by the man selling fabrics. Then I heard the scream.

A woman at the end of the read, just a few paces away from where the man had been standing, had her hand over her open mouth, shocked sobs wracking her shoulders. She pointed towards the wagons in the road. As the last wagon finally passed by and the dust began to settle, I saw a tan shape lying on the ground. The woman was pointing at a body.

Once again, I ran. I pushed past people as they began to crowd inward, flocking to the man's crumpled body like they expected it to stand up and put on a show. I knew before I was close enough to see his face who I would find. *The* man. My target.

His end had not been pleasant. Blood coated the right side of his face where a horse hoof had partly crushed his skull, and his limbs stuck out at unsuitable angles from being run over by the wagon wheels. Apparently, my rapid approach had made him desperate, and he'd tried his luck crossing the road.

"Someone should help," an English-speaking woman

in a gray tea dress and matching hat cried, averting her eyes but waving her arm in the air, drawing even more attention.

A man nearby, who might have been accompanying the English woman, shook his head. "Poor devil is beyond help."

There could be a clue on the dead man's person. Something in his pockets, hiding in his robe. I needed to search him, but people would think I was looting his body for money.

"I'll check for a pulse," I said loudly, thinking of the idea all at once.

The same man who had given up hope grumbled under his breath and looked around, as if searching for someone who could take care of the mess the man's body was making in the road.

I knelt beside the body, avoiding the blood pooling under it, my knees pressing into the warm, dusty ground. The victim's face was long but young. Very young. I paused for a moment just to wonder at how someone with so little life could have found themselves in so much trouble. Then, I remembered my own situation and mentally put the question away.

My fingers inched towards his neck while my other hand slipped between a fold in his robes. I searched blindly for no more than a few seconds before I felt soft leather. It was even easier than I'd expected. I frowned in frustration, pretending I couldn't find a good position to access his neck, and stepped over the man, moving to his other side. As my dress draped over him, one leg on either side of his body, I pulled the leather pouch from his robe and slipped it beneath my arm.

"Is he alive?" the English woman asked.

The same man huffed. "I'm telling you, he is dead. No one survives that kind of trauma."

I lightly touched the spot on the victim's neck where his pulse should have been and felt nothing. I shook my head. "He is gone."

More people gathered, and I slipped back into the crowd before turning down a side road and heading back towards the hotel where Achilles would be.

When I was far enough away to no longer attract any suspicion, I leaned against a mud brick wall and opened the leather pouch. It was simple and worn with use, and inside was a bundle of local currency and a single letter. It was written in English, confirming my suspicions that the man was not a native. I read the vaguely-worded letter three times before deciding further read throughs would offer no additional information.

I TRUST you to destroy this letter upon your first reading. I've named your target in previous correspondence and will not repeat it here. Kill him and I will send the money and name of another minister. Unlike your counterpart in Simla, use discretion. We do not need the attention now. Good luck. I will be in touch.

THERE WAS no address at the beginning, no signature at the end, and no mention of who should be murdered, but it was clear the man I'd been chasing was more than a spy in the espionage case Achilles had brought me to Tangier to investigate. I'd been chasing an assassin for hire. An international agent killing government officials for pay.

If that weren't surprising enough, the mention of Simla drew an inordinate amount of my attention. I couldn't help but let my mind flash to the last day I'd spent in Simla eight months prior, the day the car I was in exploded, killing my employers, the Beckinghams, and their daughter Rose. It was the day I'd died to my old name and claimed Rose's as my own. The day the trajectory of my life had been altered forever.

Could that all have been because of an assassin connected to the man I'd been chasing? Everyone suspected it was an incident of local terrorism—an extremist hurling a bomb at a random British official—but perhaps there was more to it. Perhaps, it hadn't been random.

I tucked the letter away and walked back towards the hotel, knowing the letter would do little to pacify Achilles. The man's death by wagon had led to a literal dead-end. Even with the letter and its possible connections to the bombing in Simla, it told us nothing about the man's identity or who his employer could be. I'd ruined my feet running through the city and it had all been for nothing.

2

Police swarmed outside the hotel, talking to one another in French, so I couldn't determine what had brought them to the scene. Whatever it was, I assumed Achilles would fill me in soon. In the moment, despite the excitement and mystery, I wanted nothing more than to blot the sweat from my brow and freshen up my makeup.

My third floor room had a window overlooking the street below, so I could look down on the officers as they paced back and forth across the grass and conferred with one another, making vague gestures towards the wing of the building where our employer had been staying. I watched them for no more than a second, thinking they looked like ants, striking out to gather a bit of information and then returning to the larger group, before I walked to the water basin in the corner.

The room lacked basic modern conveniences like an in-room sink with running water, but right now I didn't care about that. The cool water from the basin was a gift against my feverish skin, and I pressed my palms against my cheeks, hoping to absorb the coolness and carry it with me. Then, I washed what little remained of my makeup away with a dry towel and turned to the cracked oval-shaped mirror hanging on the opposite wall to reapply.

Few people asked me outright about the dent in my left cheek or the scar that stretched out from it like a spider's web, but I felt their eyes on it when they spoke to me. They looked at me like I was a ruined painting. A once beautiful thing that had been unfortunately marred. *Such a shame.* The makeup helped. It softened the harshness of the injury, forcing people to be close before they could see the full extent of it.

As I dusted on a thick layer of powder, blending out the edges, I could almost feel the pain of the explosion. The heat as everything around me evaporated in flames and smoke. With each brush stroke across my cheek, I could feel the searing warmth as the hot shrapnel burned against my skin. I rarely allowed myself to look back to that day, but when I slipped back into the memory, I could see the scene as if it was playing out in front of me all over again. Rose's mischievous smile, her hands folded in her lap, a man running towards the car, stopping traffic. And then chaos. Before I lost consciousness, I saw Rose's hand lying next to me, no longer attached to Rose. The thought gave me chills whenever I dwelt on it.

I packed away the makeup and with it, the memories. I'd had enough of death and destruction for one day. Then came a knock at the door.

Three firm raps in quick succession followed by the tapping of a foot against the thinly-carpeted hallway floor. Achilles' habits had become like an old friend to me, familiar and expected.

He pushed the door open and stepped into my room as

soon as I turned the knob. Anger rolled off of him like steam, filling the room with a thick tension that made my ears burn.

"An officer outside informed me that he saw a disheveled blonde with a scar come through the front door only a few minutes ago. I only wonder how long you planned to wait before visiting me?" Achilles marched to the window and then spun back towards me, thin arms crossed over his thin chest. Everything about him, from his body to his mustache to his patience was stretched thin.

"I'm glad he informed you I looked disheveled," I said, brushing a stray curl behind my ear. "That detail hardly seems necessary."

"At least it meant you were alive," Achilles snapped. "Do you know you were chasing a killer? A hired assassin?"

"Yes, actually—" I started, reaching for the letter hiding in the waist of my dress.

"Our employer is dead." He said the words with a serious tone that let me know I was meant to be surprised.

Truthfully, when I'd seen the robed figure jump from our employer's first-story window as Achilles and I had crossed the courtyard to his room, my hopes had not been high for our employer's survival. I'd wished for better news upon my return to the hotel, but nonetheless, I wasn't surprised.

"I found him murdered in his room, and then realized you had gone after the killer alone and undefended," he continued.

"You seem to forget this is not my first time investigating a murder, Monsieur Prideaux."

He flinched at the formal greeting, but I didn't feel anything. At one time, we'd become more comfortable with one another, but that time suddenly seemed too long ago to remember.

"You also appear to forget that I've saved your life more than once," he responded sharply. "You jump into action without thought. You put yourself and others at risk by acting impulsively. And you hinder my investigation."

I wanted to argue with him—the last point especially— but the image of the assassin bloody and crushed on the ground rose to the forefront of my mind. Achilles already believed I'd damaged his investigation, and he didn't even know the mystery man was dead yet.

Achilles ran a frustrated finger over his thin mustache, twisting the end of it in habit. "I hate to ask and encourage your behavior, but were you able to learn anything by following the man?"

I fixed my eyes on a tear in the carpet, too nervous to look him in the eyes and admit the truth. "I learned the man was an assassin hired to kill high-ranking British officials, and that he may have had some slender connection to the bombing in Simla."

Achilles drew his brows together, thoughtful. "He told you this?"

I let out a breath and shook my head. "No, I found a letter hidden in his robes."

"Hidden in his—" Achilles' voice cut off. "Is he dead?"

I glanced up at him long enough to see the color rise in his cheeks, to see his thoughtful brows turn dark and frustrated, and then looked back to the floor. "Not by any doing of my own, but yes, he is dead. A cart ran him over as he attempted to cross the street."

"To get away from you, no doubt," Achilles said. "Were you or were you not still in pursuit?"

"I was, but—"

Achilles dismissed me with a wave of his hand. "You've chased the killer to his death and left me with no one to question. Our employer is dead, and I cannot apprehend his killer."

"You call him our employer as if we knew him personally. He was a client of yours, nothing more," I said, aware I was downplaying the importance of my error. "Isn't it enough that you've solved his murder?"

"I am not being paid to solve his murder, Nellie. I was hired to uncover the espionage ring operating within the local administration, and now both my employer and my biggest lead are dead."

Hearing him use my real name jolted me back into the seriousness of my predicament. In the months I'd been with Achilles, I'd dropped my charade as Rose Beckingham ever so slightly. I only kept my false accent when we were in the company of other people, and I'd introduced myself to several people as Nellie Dennet in hopes I could reclaim my identity one day. But without Achilles by my side, I would once again be alone in the world, penniless, and without a clear path forward. As Rose, however, I would have a family and a fortune.

My parting with the London Beckinghams had been abrupt. I'd left a vague letter behind, informing them that I would not be going to New York with Catherine and Alice. Later, on arriving at Tangier, I'd contacted them again to let them know where I was and that I was safe. I had made an effort at a convincing excuse, saying I needed time away, but it felt insincere. Not exactly a burned bridge, but after the recent horror they'd been through in losing their own murderous son, my sudden departure was hardly kind. My aunt had written me recently, but I lacked the courage to read her letter. I wouldn't be surprised if she wrote to tell me they would refuse to see me again and not to call on them should I ever return to London. Though Lord and Lady Ashton had only been my aunt and uncle for eight months, the thought of being rejected by them wounded me.

Leaving with Achilles Prideaux had been a mistake.

"Did you expect the man to confess his crime and all of his connections to you?" I challenged. "Even if he were alive, what information did you expect to gather from him?"

Achilles narrowed his eyes. "Is that a criticism of my investigation?"

"Do I need to explain myself? I'm sure the world-renowned detective has never heard a criticism, so perhaps you wouldn't recognize it. Yes, it was."

Achilles opened his mouth, taking a step towards me, ready for the challenge. But then, he hesitated. Like always, he considered his next action carefully and closed his mouth. He shook his head. "We do not work well together, Nellie. We are two individuals who are more accustomed to being alone than in the company of another. I'm afraid that tendency has spoiled whatever hope there ever was of a partnership between us."

I heard the dual meaning. We would not be partners professionally or personally.

"I couldn't agree more," I said, doing my best to swallow the impulsive side of me that seemed to cause so much trouble. I wasn't sure if I really meant the words, but I needed to say them. I needed to be sensible and realistic about the fact that there was no future for us.

Shoving aside my emotions, I held the leather pouch out to him. "Here is the letter I took from the man's pocket."

Achilles opened the leather pouch carefully and pulled the letter out between two pinched fingers. He unfolded it as if he was afraid it would burst into flames. After a few quiet minutes, he refolded it and replaced it in the pouch.

"There may very well be more assassinations planned. I have to pass along this information to the British Embassy," he said, tucking the item inside of his suit jacket. "Do you mind if I keep the letter?"

I shook my head. I'd grabbed the letter in an effort to appease the anger I knew would be directed at me once Achilles realized his suspect was dead. I'd intended to give it to him all along. It was a peace offering of sorts. "It is yours."

He offered a quick bow, always the gentleman, and hurried from the room, leaving me alone once again.

I stood in the middle of the room for a moment, wondering if after eight months of floating between the two, it would be possible to split myself down the center again and decide between Nellie Dennet from New York and Rose Beckingham from London. Then, my eyes fell to the small writing desk in the corner of the room and the locked drawer where Lady Ashton's letter had been waiting for me. I unlocked the drawer and pulled out the letter before I could convince myself otherwise. The wait was over.

3

D earest Rose,

I CANNOT LIE *and say your decision to leave so suddenly did not cause Lord Ashton, Catherine, Alice, and myself a great deal of heartache, but I also must say that we understand. You, sweet Rose, have been through a terrible time. One tragedy after another seems to have befallen you, and it is no wonder you need time to yourself. I hope you know our door is always open to you, as is the offer for you to join the girls in New York.*

Catherine and Alice arrived safely after a long voyage and have begun to furnish their rooms in their aunt's home. My sister is so pleased to keep them, and though I would trust no one's watchful eye as much as yours, I believe she will keep them both out of trouble. Alice asks about you frequently, so please do write her if you have the time. She would love hearing from you.

Your letter claimed you no longer wished to lay claim on your inheritance, but instead pass on the fortune to us, and while your generosity is astounding, I hope you know we would never allow such a thing to take place. Especially after the harm my Edward caused you. We have used a small portion to pay off a few mounting bills, but otherwise, the money is yours. Lord Ashton has authorized the withdrawal of your monthly allowance from a bank there in Tangier should you have need of it. If you find yourself leaving Tangier, let us know and we can ensure you are taken care of wherever in the world you decide to call home. Though, let it be said, I hope you'll call London home again soon enough.

Love, Lady Ashton

P.S. – George sends his regards. He has resumed his duties as our driver with the utmost grace and humility despite our termination of him earlier in the year. Should you return to London, though, I believe you would once again find a loyal employee in George. And Mrs. Worthing wanted me to send along a letter from her, as well. You'll find it enclosed.

I DROPPED down into the rickety chair in front of the desk and held the letter to my chest as if to absorb the words into my very soul. I felt undeserving. Of the inheritance meant for the real Rose Beckingham and the kindness her relations had heaped upon me. A small part of me would have been relieved to find a note from the Beckinghams decrying me as a heartless woman they would no longer call niece. Then, I wouldn't have had any choice to make. I would have carried on as Nellie Dennet, making my way in the world as best I could with no family of my own and no connections. But now, I had options.

My body sagged under the weight of indecision, and I decided the day had been altogether too exhausting. I tucked Lady Ashton's letter back into the drawer along with Mrs. Worthing's letter—while I would be happy to hear from the older woman, I had no desire to read her rambling London gossip at that exact moment—and fell back onto the bed and straight to sleep.

I AWOKE to three quick knocks at the door and noticed the shadows in the room had grown longer, the light filtering through the window turning orange as the sun dipped below the horizon. Achilles had been gone awhile, and despite the several hour nap, I felt no more refreshed.

Achilles stomped into the room, his cane pounding into the floor with every step like he wished to leave indentations. "No one will listen to anything I say. I went to the embassy, but no one had heard of me. Not a soul. Can you believe it?"

It had taken me a few weeks to notice the conceit in him. The way he would flow into a room or a crime scene with no introduction and begin telling people what to do. But once I spotted it, I couldn't help but pay attention.

He continued speaking without any input from me. "The situation is now being looked at by the police as a local murder case and they do not want an '*outsider*' intruding. An outsider!"

He paced across the room several times before taking up position at the window, looking down at where the officers had been swarming earlier in the afternoon. "The only person in Tangier who regarded me as a great detective was the government minister who hired me. And who is now dead. So, with no way to communicate with the local government, I believe it would be best for the two of us to return to London where my reputation is better-known. There, I will be able to warn the authorities of an assassination plot and be taken seriously."

I'd woken up from my nap without a decision but listening to Achilles talk about returning to London seemed to solidify something inside of me I hadn't been consciously aware of. I knew what I wanted to do, what I needed to do. It suddenly felt obvious.

"I believe, Monsieur Prideaux, that it would be best for *you* to return to London alone," I said, reclaiming the fake British accent I'd used as Rose Beckingham. Though I hadn't used it in a few weeks, the lilt of the words came back to me naturally, as if I'd never stopped.

Achilles raised an eyebrow at the sudden change, studying me for a moment. "You do not wish to join me, Rose?"

He hadn't called me Rose in several weeks, either, and I could tell it took effort for him to revert back to the habit.

I shook my head. "It isn't that, exactly, Achilles. It is simply that I feel pulled in another direction. You wish to warn the officials of the plot to assassinate high-ranking officials, which I believe is a right and noble cause, but that is a task you can do alone. There is no place for me in the mission. So, I believe travelling to India once more would be a better use of my time and abilities."

"You have no plan to return to London, then?" he asked in a tone I couldn't read.

"Not at present," I said. "The letter I discovered this morning made mention of a similar attack in Simla. After the explosion last summer and my recovery afterward, I was rushed away secretly and placed on a boat to Europe without any time to process what had happened or discover the truth. I would like to go back to the place where it happened and come to know the events that lead to the deaths of 'my parents' and my companion, Nellie Dennet."

Achilles pressed his lips together until they were pale white and as thin as his mustache. "You would rather carry on in your charade? You'd rather play Rose Beckingham than be yourself? Is that your true aim in taking up this accent and going back to India, starting your life over once again?"

"I'm surprised that after so much time with me, you are not glad for me to be playing someone else. Though you may deny it, Achilles, you grew rather tired of Nellie Dennet's company." I smiled at him, hoping it looked warmer than it felt. "And my true aim is to unravel the mystery of what happened that day in Simla. The evidence may be scattered and long past being useful, but if the Beckinghams were killed by an assassin like the man who killed your employer, for reasons it turns out had nothing to do with local politics, then I feel it is important to know who ordered and carried out their deaths and why."

Achilles made no move to respond to my claim that he had become tired of my company, he simply shook his head. "You cannot go to India alone. Especially to Simla. Someone there sought to kill the Beckinghams for a reason. If you return, there is no guarantee you will be safe."

"You brought me to Tangier as your partner knowing we would be in frequent danger. Forgive me, but I do not see the difference."

"You are not alone, first," he said, holding up a finger to make his point. "But I also brought you along under the belief that most of the danger in our investigation would be from petty criminals, not highly-organized and skilled international assassins. Frankly, you are out of your depth."

I thought of how many times my life had been threatened in the preceding eight months, how many times I had faced death and walked away unharmed and couldn't help but, yet again, disagree with Monsieur Prideaux.

"Frankly, that is my decision to make," I said sternly.

Achilles took a step towards me, twisting his cane back and forth into the floor like he was squishing a bug with it. "I brought you with me to Morocco because I thought I was protecting you. I thought it was an offer of a new life free from the charade of being Rose Beckingham. Of course, I now see I have only succeeded in introducing you to a greater danger neither of us fully understand yet. So, you may resume the charade of being Rose Beckingham if you like where you will be free to enjoy the wealth and ease of being a Beckingham. But do so back in London."

Achilles truly was a handsome man. His face sagged after a busy day, the skin beneath his eyes gray and sunken, but he had a warmth to his skin that spoke to his many exotic adventures around the world, and his eyes sparkled with secrets. It was what had drawn me to him from the start. That and his faith in me when so many others saw me as a broken girl picking herself up after tragedy.

"You once told me I'd make a fine private detective like yourself," I said, clasping my hands tightly together in front of me. "Do you still feel that way?"

He ran a hand across his forehead, wiping away sweat that wasn't there. "You have a talent for observation that no one can deny, but you walk too willingly into danger. If I'd realized that, I would never have encouraged your fascination with crime. I regret involving you in this and placing you in the way of danger."

I pulled my lips into a tight smile. "Thank you for your honesty, Monsieur Prideaux. When do we leave for London?"

His eyebrows raised in surprise before he collected himself. "Two days is the soonest we'll be able to leave. I intend to lay low and remain discrete until then."

THE DOOR to my room closed with a thud behind me, and I hesitated in the hallway, holding my breath to see if I'd woken anyone. I heard nothing in the hallway or behind the door next to mine, the room where Achilles Prideaux had been sleeping for the past two weeks since arriving in Tangier. When I felt confident no one was coming for me, I firmly gripped my small case of belongings and moved carefully down the hallway, avoiding the squeaky spots in the floor.

I'd allowed Achilles to believe he'd convinced me to return to London because I knew I would not be free of him otherwise. For reasons unknown, he'd made himself my caretaker, ending any opportunity of our friendship and partnership turning into anything more, and making me feel like a caged animal. If I returned to London with Achilles, he would have deposited me at my aunt and uncle's house like a parcel. He'd led me to believe he valued my opinion and my abilities, but I had come to see that he viewed me as a child to be watched and protected, incapable of determining her own destiny. Achilles believed the investigation had become too dangerous for me, and that was apparently the end of the discussion. He intended to leave me in London while he went back to working the international assassin case by himself. And while I had no issue with him working the more official end of the investigation, I refused to be pushed out simply because he thought he could handle the risks and I couldn't.

So, just as I'd told Achilles earlier, my sights were set on India. I'd made a few enquiries and learned that a ship set sail from port in the morning. Wherever it was bound, I planned to be on it. From there, I would make my way to India.

The night was still dark, and the ship wouldn't set sail for many hours yet, but I knew if I'd waited until the morning, Achilles would have stopped me or followed me onto the boat. And in many ways, having him along for the trip to India would have been worse than not going at all. The attack in Simla was personal, not just another case for him to dissect and solve. It had disrupted my life in the cruelest way, and if the believed terrorist attack was actually a planned assassination, I wanted to find out for myself.

The real Rose Beckingham deserved justice, and so did I.

4
———

I was grateful for Lady Ashton's letter encouraging me to once again take up the mantle of Rose. I'd been afraid I may have burned bridges in departing London so abruptly and without a proper goodbye, but she'd offered me endless grace and the return of my inheritance, which had come into use sooner than I ever would have guessed.

I wandered the dark streets of Tangier, keeping careful watch for anyone who might have been following me, Achilles or otherwise, until the bank opened. Then, I pulled out the funds my uncle had freed for me and walked directly to the ticket office to buy passage to India. I sent a letter to my Aunt and Uncle, informing them they would next hear word from me in Bombay in hopes they would be kind enough to make funds available to me there, as well. Then, I boarded the ship and set sail, leaving Achilles Prideaux and Tangier behind.

∾

THE VOYAGE WAS UNEVENTFUL, which pleased me to no end. I

had more than enough time to plan what I would do upon arriving in India, and I was able to grow completely comfortable again with the accent and mannerisms of Rose by practicing on the other passengers on board. Since no one knew anything of Rose Beckingham or the trouble that had befallen her, my behavior was scrutinized even more closely—people were more wary of strangers than a familiar name. And it seemed my performance drew no noticeable looks or attention.

As soon as the ship docked at my ultimate destination I retrieved my luggage and went to the nicest hotel in Bombay —only the best for Miss Rose Beckingham—and secured a room for myself. Unlike the small room in Tangier, my new suite had a paned window with a built-in seat that I could sit in to look down at the garden below. There was also a four-poster bed with silk sheets, and a separate sitting room with velvet sofas and sliding wooden doors for privacy.

I'd only been in the hotel for a few hours when there was a knock on my door. Crossing the room and answering it, I half-expected to find Monsieur Prideaux on the other side, having hunted me down after I'd left Tangier in secret. It had been so long since I'd been friendly with anyone else, that I couldn't imagine who would want to see me.

But instead of a tall, thin Frenchman, I opened the door to discover a short English woman with gray hair.

"Rose Beckingham," she said, her tone flat and sure.

"Yes?" I asked, glancing up and down the hallway for some clue as to why I was being called upon and why the woman already knew my name. Her clothing spoke to a higher-class, so she didn't work at the hotel, but I couldn't turn her away merely for being a stranger. For one thing, the hunch in her spine made me worry she would topple over if I closed the door too hard.

Her wrinkled brow drew together in a mixture of concern and embarrassment. "You may not remember. I'm not sure we ever met, but I was friends with your mother."

My mother? Being out of practice, it took me a few seconds to gather that the woman was referencing Mrs. Beckingham, Rose's mother. "My mother," I repeated enthusiastically before turning my face down in a frown.

The old woman matched my expression. "I was devastated to hear of the accident, and then absolutely overjoyed to learn of your remarkable escape."

"Thank you for your thoughts..." I paused, realizing I still didn't know who I was speaking to.

"Mrs. Hutchins."

"Thank you, Mrs. Hutchins," I finished, smiling in thanks and apology. I reached out to grasp the woman's wrinkled hand in my own, but as soon as I moved towards her, she sprang back faster than I would have thought possible.

I retracted my hand immediately, tucking it against my side. "I'm sorry. I didn't meant to startle you—"

"Your mother was aware of my peculiarities, but the information may not have ever been passed to you, as it wasn't necessary at the time," Mrs. Hutchins began to explain, her eyes still wide and watching like I might reach out for her again unprompted. I wished I could assure her I would do no such thing, not after her reaction. "I do my best to avoid physical contact. Disease can spread in many ways, and I prefer to minimize my exposure."

I nodded. Did I look diseased?

"Oh, yes. I do remember that now," I lied. "Mother spoke fondly of you on many occasions, Mrs. Hutchins."

"Florence, if you'd rather," she said, smiling at the compliment. "Your mother called me 'Flo' more than once, and several of our friends still use that name. It never fails to make me think of her."

"I'm so glad you came to see me, Florence," I said as sweetly as I could. "But I just got off the boat a few hours ago. I am so pleased to speak with you, but how did you learn I was in the city so quickly?"

"Oh," Mrs. Hutchins said, her face lighting up with realization. "Your aunt and uncle contacted a few of your mother and father's friends when they received word you would be returning to India. Lord and Lady Ashton wanted to ensure you would have acquaintances in India and would be made to feel welcome."

Internally, I groaned. How many more similar run-ins would I face? And would I be able to fool all of them into believing I was Rose? She and I had always looked alike— similar build, coloring, and hairstyle—but unlike Rose's acquaintances in London who had not seen her in ten years, the people in India had seen Rose as early as eight months ago. Not to mention, a few of them had seen me, as well. My clothes were rags compared to my closet now, and I did not have the scar or makeup then, but still, the likelihood of being recognized and my deception uncovered were greater than I had realized.

"My aunt and uncle are unendingly kind," I said, forcing a smile. "I'm so glad they thought of me."

"What is the reason for your return?" Mrs. Hutchins asked. "I only inquire because we all heard your closest relations were in London, so without your father's work, I couldn't imagine what would lure you back to India."

I couldn't very well tell her I was there investigating the possibility that the Beckinghams had been killed by a hired assassin who may very well kill another high-ranking British official in the near future. That information was not only secret, but highly suspicious. No one would expect Rose to be doing her own detective work. In an ironic twist, it would be far more likely she would have hired someone like Achilles Prideaux for the job.

"I'm here for a kind of pilgrimage," I said, thinking fast. "I'd like to return to the place where the attack occurred to try and find closure."

Mrs. Hutchins gave me a sympathetic frown and nodded before taking a deep breath and returning to happier topics of conversation. "If Simla is your destination, then I hope you'll allow us the privilege of accompanying you so you do not have to travel alone. Travel can be dangerous for a beautiful young woman."

"I do not want to be a burden," I said, dismissing her offer with a wave and smiling. "I am accustomed to travelling by myself and do not have any fears."

"It would not be a burden," she insisted. "Arthur, my son, and I are already planning to head into the hills to escape the oppressive heat of the summer. We are far from the hottest month, and I am already sweltering. By going with us, you would just be putting an old woman's mind at ease. Really, I must insist."

Rose had never gone anywhere by herself, which was partly why I'd been hired as her companion. She enjoyed conversation and male admirers more than most, so refusing Mrs. Hutchins and her son would be out of character. There didn't seem to be any choice but to accept the offer.

"Well, if I would be putting you at ease, then that is all that is important," I said. "I would love to travel with you both."

Mrs. Hutchins left shortly after I agreed, promising to be in touch, and I wondered if it would be possible to slip away

as I had from Monsieur Prideaux in Tangier. Would Mrs.
Hutchins be alarmed if I did not meet them on the train
platform in two days? Or would she assume I'd had little
interest in her offer and let it go? My instincts told me she
was the kind of woman to fuss, which meant she would alert
everyone in town to my absence, and my return to Bombay
and intention to visit Simla would be even more widely
circulated than it apparently had been already. The safest
option, unfortunately, was to join Florence and her son, and
pray I could soon extricate myself from their company.

I ARRIVED at the train platform shortly before the train was
set to depart and found Mrs. Hutchins leaning against a
newspaper stand and fanning herself with the front head-
lines. Pink color was high in her cheeks and neck, and she
looked in desperate need of sitting down. The middle-aged
man standing next to her, who I assumed was her son based
on the similarities between their size and stature, tapped his
foot impatiently against the brick platform, his eyes
searching every face that passed with an air of impatience.
Next to him was a man Mrs. Hutchins had not told me to
expect. He was short and thin, his face gaunt like he had
skipped too many meals and his head balding. And unlike
Mrs. Hutchins, he was white as marble.

Arthur Hutchins' careful eyes fell on me when I was still
far away, and he turned to his mother and whispered something in her ear. She turned her pink, shiny face towards me
immediately and waved, though the simple gesture looked
like it took her a great deal of effort. I waved back and sped
up to close the distance between us.

"I'm sorry to keep you waiting," I said, not being entirely

truthful. Part of me had hoped I'd arrive too late to board this train and would have to travel to Simla alone.

"We weren't waiting," Mrs. Hutchins said. "We were just soaking in the last bit of fresh air before we board. This is my son, Arthur."

"Glad you made it," Arthur said, his tone conveying something of annoyance, despite his mother's assurance they hadn't been waiting on me.

"Thank you for accompanying me," I said. "I was relieved when your mother made the offer. I did not wish to travel alone."

The idea of making the journey alone actually sounded perfect, and I mourned that which I'd never have while Mrs. Hutchins continued the introductions.

"And this," she said, gesturing to the pale man standing next to Arthur, "is Arthur's private secretary, Mr. Charles Barlow."

Mr. Barlow pulled his lips together into a tight pucker like he'd just licked a lemon and nodded his head to me, giving me the full view of his crescent-shaped head of hair. "Pleased to meet you, Miss Beckingham."

"Mr. Barlow recently returned from a vacation of his own and is now accompanying us on our getaway. Isn't that funny?" Mrs. Hutchins asked, smiling as though she'd just told a hilarious joke. I smiled out of kindness, but neither Mr. Barlow or her son felt the need to be kind.

After waiting a few hopeful seconds in the expectation that the men would acknowledge her words, she opened her mouth to say something else, but Arthur cut her off immediately. "Now that we are all here, perhaps we should take our seats?"

The question didn't leave any room for dissenting opinions, and I could tell he wanted to make it abundantly clear to me for a second time that I had held up the proceedings. I refused to allow him to fluster me.

"Absolutely," I agreed with a wide smile.

Arthur grabbed his mother's luggage and his own and headed for the train, followed by his mother. I stepped back to allow Mr. Barlow to follow his employer, but he shook his head, fixed his eyes on me and bowed unnecessarily low, one arm extended outward. "After you, Miss Beckingham."

I realized that for better or worse, it could be put off no longer. I really was on my way back to the place where it had all begun.

Mr. and Mrs. Hutchins, though a son and mother pair, bickered like any married couple I'd ever known. Mrs. Hutchins insisted she was feeling ill, too hot, or crowded at least once every five minutes, to which her son would respond with a sharp reply that quieted her only until the next thing went wrong. Mr. Barlow seemed unfazed by his employer's arguing, his face remaining a perfectly neutral mask throughout the entire trip. At first, I found it disturbing that he could be so unresponsive and immune to the constant complaints and arguing, but as one day turned to two and then three, I found him inspiring. I wanted to kneel at his feet and have him teach me his techniques. I'd been held at gunpoint multiple times in my life yet accepting Mrs. Hutchins' travel offer quickly became my biggest regret.

Staring out the window proved to be the only method of escape. I watched as burning hot plains that stretched into the horizon blended seamlessly into the tree-covered

Himalayan foothills, peaks and valleys filling in the land-scape in a way that was both familiar and breathtaking.

We switched trains as the altitude increased, moving higher into the mountains, closer to the hill station of Simla. Our train passed by mountain towns set just off of cliffs like they could be pushed right over the edge, and when we rounded one mountain, a wall of rock opening onto a full view of a range of mountains, snow-capped and tall as the sky, even Mr. and Mrs. Hutchins had to stop arguing to take notice.

The sight helped to soften the memories of India and Simla, in particular, that I'd been holding onto. What I'd told Mrs. Hutchins about coming to Simla for closure had been a lie, but I found myself thinking I could inadvertently find closure as well as solve an international assassin mystery. There was no reason I couldn't do both.

"I do hope you won't feel nervous joining in activities in the community," Mrs. Hutchins said as we neared out final destination. Even she had grown weary of complaining about the lack of space to stretch her legs and had moved on to other topics.

I knew that by "the community" she meant the British officers, government officials, and their wives and children, who made up society in the hill town.

"I look forward to it," I said, although I secretly had little intention of joining in on any activities. I had a mission, and it did not involve attending parties or government dinners. I'd listened to Rose describe enough of them when I was a servant for the Beckinghams that I knew exactly how dull they could be. The last summer we had spent in Simla—the same summer the Beckinghams were murdered—Rose had feigned an illness most of the summer to avoid such events. I was then always at her side, where she taught me to perfect her accent and how to dress like a lady. I had no idea at the time how important those lessons would come to be.

Rose's past absence at social occasions would now prove to be helpful in maintaining my disguise. Many acquaintances did not see her at all that summer, meaning it had now been nearly two years since they would have seen her. That timeframe would hopefully excuse any obvious differences in appearance between Rose and me.

"I know you are coming to Simla with a purpose, but it is good for a young woman to socialize," Mrs. Hutchins said.

"I'm sure Miss Beckingham has her own plans," Arthur said. It was the first time during the entire trip that I'd liked him.

"I only wish to help her feel included," Mrs. Hutchins whispered, as though I were not sitting directly across from her, able to hear every word.

Desperate for anything to take my mind off the last few hours of the trip, I pulled out the letter from my aunt I'd had hiding in my desk drawer in Tangier and removed the second letter she had enclosed from Mrs. Worthing. At one point, I'd found Mrs. Worthing's company unbearable, but I now wished more than anything she and her husband were accompanying me to Simla. Her silly gossip and the loving banter between she and her husband was much preferable to the negativity exuded by the Hutchins.

Lovely Rose,

I hope you'll forgive this hasty note. I'm writing it quickly in order to include it with a letter your aunt said she would be sending you, and I do hope I can be brief so it will make it in time.

Mr. Worthing and I miss you terribly. When we agreed to travel with you from Simla to London that fateful summer, I had no idea how dear you would become to me. I look upon you like a daughter, but I must insist you do not look upon me as a mother. It would make me feel far too old. Mr. Worthing says it would make me feel my age, but we are not concerning ourselves with what he thinks.

Aseem has settled in nicely as an invaluable servant. He does more than he is asked and always with a positive attitude. I intend to keep the boy hired on as long as he will stay.

I do hope you are taking care of yourself wherever in the world you are. Morocco, I believe your aunt said. I've never been, so you must write and tell me what it is like. When you come back to London, please visit. We have so much to tell you.

WITH LOVE,
   Mrs. and Mr. Worthing

I DETERMINED at once that no matter how busy I became with the investigation, I would sit down and reestablish my connections with everyone from Rose's life. I would write to Mr. and Mrs. Worthing, thanking them for all they'd done for me up to that point. I'd write to Lord and Lady Ashton to inform them of my safe arrival and my gratitude for their undeserved kindness, and I'd write to my cousins in New York to apologize for not accompanying them there.

Finally, after months of uncertainly, I was committed to being Rose Beckingham, and I intended to do it properly.

5

———

Somewhere along the way, although the exact details had become fuzzy to me, I'd agreed to stay in a rented bungalow at the edge of town with the Hutchins. I'd agreed to the details prior to actually becoming well acquainted with either Mrs. Hutchins or her son, and certainly before I'd spent any time with them together. By the time we arrived in Simla and took a car to the bungalow, I questioned whether I shouldn't send word to Achilles Prideaux and tell him I'd changed my mind about accompanying him to London.

The car seemed to move steadily upward until I didn't believe we could go any higher. Then, it would climb higher still. Timbered houses lined the winding roads and nestled themselves amongst the foliage. I knew that the smaller dwellings lower down the hill were the homes of native locals, while the larger buildings clustered higher up were where the people Mrs. Hutchins referred to as "society" stayed during the warm months.

The altitude was so great that everything sat against a

background of pure white clouds. Thick greenery and flower gardens stood in opposition to the dry, dusty cities further South, making it possible to forget we were in India at all.

"I can hardly tell what is worse," Mrs. Hutchins wheezed, drawing my attention from a particularly lovely arrangement of rose bushes. "The claustrophobic heat of Bombay or the thin air of Simla. Is anyone else struggling to breathe?"

"Every second," Arthur said, his voice drawn long and lazy.

"You'll become accustomed to it," Mr. Barlow said.

Mrs. Hutchins shook her head. "I could never become accustomed to air this thin. Simla is for the young. My days here are numbered."

Her dreary talk carried on until we pulled to a stop in front of the bungalow. It had a low, wide front porch with timber beams that stretched from the ground to the roof. The size was just large enough to comfortably accommodate the four of us, as well as the servants I understood came with the house.

The room allotted to me was at the back with a single window that looked out over a garden. I would have liked a view of the mountains, but I was pleased to be far away from the main rooms where Mrs. Hutchins' complaining continued, as she talked of dust gathered on the furniture and the moist air that would surely ruin her already ailing lungs.

I HAD little time to settle in and supervise the servants' unpacking of my luggage. The day was already half spent and darkness came soon after dinner. It was a strange feeling, passing my first night in this place, so close to the location of last summer's horrible events. Putting aside fears of snakes or other unwelcome visitors, I opened my window wide to the night breeze and trusted to the curtain of fine netting that encircled my bed to protect me from nighttime insects. I fell asleep counting the stars twinkling outside the window.

Word of our arrival must have spread quickly, for the next day we already had guests at the house. I returned from a late morning walk around the property where I breathed in "the dangerously thin air," in time to see the newcomers drive up.

A young man in a British soldier's uniform exited the vehicle and extended a hand to help an elegant red-headed woman out after him. As the couple made their way to the door where Mr. Hutchins was standing to greet them, a rare smile on his face, a blonde gentleman stepped from the back of the car, as well. He also wore a uniform, though his seemed noticeably more distinguished, decorated with patches and pins. He heard my feet on the gravel and turned towards me, bowing.

"Are you with the Hutchins' or a guest at today's festivities?" he asked in a baritone voice.

"Neither." I smiled, extending a hand to him. "Or both, perhaps. I am staying in the bungalow with Mrs. Hutchins and her son, though I scarcely know them. And seeing as I had no prior knowledge of any such festivities, I may not be an invited guest."

The man tilted his head to the side, a wide smile spreading his lips thin and drawing attention to his thin mustache that was not unlike the one I'd so detested on

Monsieur Prideaux's face, though this one was blonde rather than black. "I am unaccompanied today, so you are welcome to say you are arriving with me if anyone gives you any trouble."

The flirtation in his voice was unmistakable.

"And who shall I name as my companion?" I asked.

He bowed again. "Forgive me. Lieutenant Graham Collins."

"Rose Beckingham," I introduced myself.

Recognition of my name flashed across his face as he glanced towards my cheek where the scar was likely obvious in the midday sun, but his startled expression was replaced with a smile in a second. I wondered how many times I would earn a similar reaction during my time in Simla. It had only been eight months since the bombing, and I doubted sensational news like that would fade into memory after such a short amount of time.

The Lieutenant stayed close to my side as we passed Arthur Hutchins at the door. Mr. Hutchins smiled at the Lieutenant and offered the surliest of grimaces to me, and walked into the dining room. Since I'd had breakfast that morning, the table had been set with three additional place settings and a large bouquet of flowers from the garden had been brought in, filling the room with a lovely scent.

Mrs. Hutchins introduced me to the two people I'd seen getting out of the car in front of the Lieutenant, Mr. James Clarke and Miss Jane Dayes. Mr. Clarke seemed more interested in the food than in any actual conversation and Miss Dayes passed the time by complimenting every single detail of the table and room several times over, until even Mrs. Hutchins looked weary of thanking her. The conversation was stilted, which I attributed to Mrs. Hutchins' lunch guests being at least four decades younger than she was. Even her middle-aged son had little in common with the guests. But as conversation revealed, Miss Dayes was the daughter of a government official who had once offered Mrs. Hutchins a favor of some kind, and she'd felt it necessary to repay his kindness by subjecting his daughter to an uncomfortable meal.

Admittedly, my attention was fixed on a large window looking into a central atrium filled with a stone garden and several small plants. The conversation at the table, even that of the handsome Lieutenant, could not hold my interest. I wanted to go into the marketplace in Simla where the attack on the Beckinghams—and myself—had occurred. I wanted to see the place where it had happened and attempt to relive the memories I had spent eight months repressing. The bomber's face had always been a mystery to me, a gap in my otherwise crystal-clear memory. I could recall the scent of singed skin, the sizzle of the car's upholstery, the color of the dust in the air. But not the face of the man who had so altered my life.

The door from the kitchen opened and Mr. Barlow appeared, looking as gray and lifeless as ever, despite the beautiful day. He took in the table with a cool eye, stopping on every face including mine, and then bent down to whisper in Mr. Hutchins' ear. As soon as the message was delivered, Mr. Hutchins nodded, and Mr. Barlow left. I couldn't imagine what kind of message Mr. Hutchins could receive that would be important enough to interrupt a meal, but more than that, I couldn't imagine being the person who delivered those messages. Mr. Barlow's job as the private secretary to the perpetually sour-faced Mr. Hutchins had to be a source of anguish, and suddenly, I could understand why he looked so grim and lifeless. In a position such as his, I wouldn't have found much joy, either.

"Were you acquainted with the General, Lieutenant Collins?" Mrs. Hutchins asked, interrupting Miss Dayes in the middle of a long-winded compliment about the meal.

The Lieutenant's mustache flicked in a peculiar way that caused me to take notice.

"Who do you mean, Ma'am?" Lieutenant Collins asked.

"Surely, the lady is talking about General Thomas Hughes," Miss Dayes said in a loud whisper, as though she were letting the table in on the secret, but attempting to keep it away from someone in the other room.

"Who is Thomas Hughes?" I asked, unable to contain the question. The conversation had thus far been very uninspiring, and I was in desperate need of some kind of stimulation. Anything worth whispering about during lunch conversation was worth my notice, surely.

"Our Rose just arrived in the country a few days ago," Mrs. Hutchins said by way of explaining my ignorance. "She was in Morocco, I believe she said. Is that right, dear? Morocco?"

I nodded impatiently, turning to the Lieutenant for an explanation.

He turned towards me, his face pulled taut like a canvas stretched too tight over a frame. "General Thomas Hughes was a soldier stationed in Simla for the summer. He passed away last week."

"Oh, that's horrible," I said, deflating slightly. Discussing the death of a man I didn't know was not the scintillating conversation I'd been searching for.

Miss Dayes leaned forward to look past her companion, Mr. Clarke, who was on his third piece of chicken with no sign of slowing. "If you'll forgive me Lieutenant, you left out the detail that the man hanged himself in a public place."

Intriguing.

"Is that right?" I covered my mouth with my hand, feigning shock. The death was horrible and surprising to be sure, but I'd seen enough in the previous eight months that little could truly shock me anymore. I turned to the Lieutenant. "I can understand why you might have left out such a detail. If you knew the man, I'm sure it is difficult to recall such facts."

The Lieutenant sat up straighter. "Returning to Mrs. Hutchins' original question, I actually did not know the General personally. I'm sure we crossed paths once or twice, but we were not acquaintances. I learned of his death at the same time as everyone else."

"He hanged himself in the reading room of a club," Miss Dayes continued. I was very pleased to learn that when she wasn't spending all her time on useless compliments, she was quite the gossip. "It is surprising someone didn't walk in while he was setting up the rope. How he managed to go through with it undisturbed is a wonder."

I furrowed my brow. "It is unusual for a suicide to happen in public. Most people reserve such things for the privacy of their own dwellings."

Mrs. Hutchins curled her lip and shook her head. "It's a nasty business. Unforgivable in a spiritual sense, I say."

"Surely the man endured something great in order to resort to such a measure," I said, defending the deceased man's soul while also fishing for details.

"I'd never heard of the man before learning of his death," Mrs. Hutchins said.

Miss Dayes shook her head. "My father mentioned

knowing the name, but otherwise, I have no connection to him."

The Lieutenant felt my eyes on him and sighed. "I also know nothing of him. His death remains a mystery to everyone I have talked to. Those who did know him say he was a pleasant man in good spirits."

Mr. Hutchins and Mr. Clarke continued eating as though no one else was even at the table, and I sagged slightly in resignation. I was in Simla on personal business, but I couldn't help but wish there had been more info on the man's death. Perhaps, Achilles Prideaux was right about me. I couldn't go anywhere without finding a bit of trouble.

"In happier news," the Lieutenant said, turning to me. "Myself, Mr. Clarke, and Miss Dayes have plans to take a picnic to some ancient ruins tomorrow if you would like to join, Miss Beckingham?"

"That would be lovely," Mrs. Hutchins said, clapping her hands together.

Lieutenant Collins quirked his lips to one side of his mouth for a second, clearly displeased at the thought of the mother-son duo tagging along on our outing. But then he turned to her with a smile. "Of course, you and your son are also more than welcome to join us, Mrs. Hutchins."

The woman waved him away. "I have little desire to be out of doors more than necessary, Lieutenant. But you are kind to invite us. Isn't he kind, Arthur?"

Her son turned to her and gave a nod that thinly veiled his apathy.

I briefly debated turning the man down. I wanted to get into the marketplace as soon as possible, but I also knew little of the area. Although I'd spent just as much time in Simla as the Beckinghams, I didn't know the place as well.

My attention was always on Rose, so I had little energy left for sight-seeing or meeting people beyond the immediate family. Having a few of my own connections in the city could be beneficial to my search for the perpetrator of the attack.

"I would love nothing more than to talk with you all further," I said, looking down the table at Mr. Clarke, who was still eating, and Miss Dayes. When I finally turned to the Lieutenant, I couldn't ignore the sparkle in his eyes, or the way it reminded me of a particular Frenchman. Something in my stomach clenched at the memory, but I pressed it down and smiled back at him.

THE RUINS the Lieutenant mentioned were so near the Hutchins' bungalow we could have walked, but we chose instead to take a car. It was a short drive, but long enough that I exhausted all possible conversation topics with Mr. Clarke and Miss Dayes. The two of them took to canoodling together in the seat—so close that I thought Mr. Clarke would crush the paper flower adorning the waist of Miss Dayes' dress—their fingers entwined with one another. Miss Dayes pointed out the window at every landmark as we passed it, acting as though she'd never seen the world through the window of a car before. I had no issue with ignoring her and her beau completely, instead focusing on Lieutenant Collins, who was already proving to be a great connection to have in Simla.

"The theater is a good way to spend an afternoon," he said, tilting his head to the side like he wasn't sure. "The screen flickers in and out sometimes, but it is a cool place to go during the heat of the day. Though, if you can attend, the polo matches are also great fun. The young soldiers are not properly trained in the sport, but the crowd never seems to mind."

"And do you compete in the game?" I asked.

"Do I strike you as a young soldier?" he asked, blonde eyebrows raised. "I would fall off the horse and break a hip, I fear."

I smiled and pursed my lips. "I'd say as much about Arthur Hutchins, perhaps, but I believe you would make good competition for a good number of young men."

His mustache twitched in a smile. "You better be careful with your tone, Miss Beckingham, or I'll take that as a compliment."

"Please do!" I said. "It was meant as one."

I worried the Lieutenant was already a bit too ensnared by my flirtatious tone, but he seemed to me the kind of man who, unlike his companion Miss Dayes, did not gossip openly with those he only slightly knew. If I wanted his help finding out information, he would have to trust me as a friend. So, a friend was what I intended to be. If he mistook my kindness as intentions towards a relationship of another kind, then that couldn't be helped.

The site was an intricately carved stone temple, dedicated to the Hindu deity Hanuman. Colonnades with cloverleaf archways ran down both sides of a wide courtyard, and crumbling stone stairs led from the walkway to a grassy area in the center. Miss Dayes pulled on her soldier's hand until he followed her into the grass where they spread out a blanket. Lieutenant Collins and I trailed behind them, our hands pressed firmly to our sides.

"Have you had the opportunity to visit any of your friends since you've been in the city?" he asked.

"I do not have many friends here. I only came into town a few days ago," I reminded him.

"But this is not your first time in Simla, correct?" he asked. Then, he looked apologetic. "I have no desire to remind you of worse times, but I've heard your name before in connection with the city."

I was so accustomed to talking to Londoners who only knew Rose Beckingham as a little girl that I was not prepared for what it would be like to meet people who knew her or knew of her shortly before her death. It was a reminder that I needed to be much more thoughtful in my responses.

"Yes," I said, nodding slowly. "You do not need to worry. I'm well aware many people heard of the accident when it happened and will remember my name still."

The Lieutenant slowed his pace, allowing more time to converse before we reached the couple ahead of us who were opening a wicker basket and lying out our lunch of cold meats and cheeses with ripe fruits. "I was in Simla at the time, Miss. Everyone was heartbroken for you and your family. I'm sure it was a devastating time. Shortly after everything happened, I found myself wishing to reach out to you and offer condolences, but I was not an acquaintance of you or your family, so I thought it would be intrusive. Then, I heard you left the city, and no one expected you to return. Imagine my surprise when I ran into you by pure happenstance yesterday."

"A happy coincidence amongst sad circumstances," I said, offering him a smile.

It could have been the light or the warmth of the day, but I thought I noticed a blush creeping into the Lieutenant's face. "If we do not hurry, I fear Mr. Clarke may eat the picnic lunch for himself."

I laughed. "He has an appetite to be sure."

"Enough for him and three other men." Lieutenant

Collins shook his head and offered me his arm, leading me down the stairs and across the grass.

After lunch, Miss Dayes dragged the food-weary Mr. Clarke up and down the stairs and through the arches, stopping every so often to pose in front of the architecture as though she were the star in a film. Lieutenant Collins and I stayed on the blanket, watching as our companions explored the ancient site.

"Why have you come back to Simla?"

The question surprised me, and I turned to the Lieutenant with a puzzled expression on my face, as though I hadn't heard him, though I certainly had. "Excuse me?"

"I'm sure my manners are unforgivable, bringing up your life's tragedy twice on the same outing, but I only wonder why you came back to this place?"

"I've met many unforgiveable men, and you are not one of them, Lieutenant."

He smiled at me, his blonde mustache turning up on one side.

"But to answer your question," I said, glad for an excuse to dive back into the subject. Now that the Lieutenant had mentioned the bombing twice in the same afternoon, I could ask him for my favor without fear of him being suspicious of my motives. "I came back to Simla to find a measure of closure for myself. The last eight months have been difficult"—more physically than emotionally, considering the murder cases I had been involved in, but the Lieutenant did not need to know that— "and I hoped coming back to the place where my family was murdered would grant some kind of spiritual peace."

Lieutenant Collins nodded, his eyebrows drawn together. "You left the city so quickly after the attack. I'm sure being back here will help, if only in the smallest sense."

I shrugged my shoulder and pinched the soft fabric of my rose-colored tea gown between my fingers. My legs were tucked up underneath me, and I was propped up on one arm on the blanket, leaning towards Lieutenant Collins. It all seemed very familiar. To anyone walking by, we probably looked like a couple, the same as Mr. Clarke and Miss Dayes. Well, not exactly the same, because we were not holding hands and running around the ancient temple like escaped children, but we looked friendly with one another. I hoped we were friendly.

"It has given me a slight comfort to be in the last place I spent with my family. The memories are hiding around every corner, though there is one memory I have been desperate to reclaim but can't seem to conjure."

Lieutenant Collins raised his brows in a question.

"I cannot see the perpetrator's face," I said, my voice low. "I know I saw him seconds before the attack, but his features have been wiped from my mind like a drawing in the sand. It is quite frustrating."

"It seems best that you not recall him at all," the Lieutenant said. "He is not worthy of a space inside your head."

I nodded slowly. "You may be right, but that information does not make my desire to see him any less. I think putting a face to the memory would help me to view the monster as a man rather than a demon. I think it would allow me to move on from the incident in a way I have not been able to these past eight months."

Lieutenant Collins leaned back on his hands and turned his face to the blue sky. He was quite a handsome man, his jaw strong and pronounced, blue eyes bright and deep. In another life, I would have grabbed his hand and pulled him behind me the way Miss Dayes did with her beau. I would have giggled when he spoke and done my best to catch his eye in a crowd. In this life, however, more important matters hung over every situation like clouds heavy with rain, demanding my immediate attention lest I be caught in the downpour.

Finally, the Lieutenant turned his eyes to me. They were kind—adoring, even—and part of me felt a little guilty at the idea that the man had been caught so easily in my kindness and attention. I knew he would do whatever I asked.

"And you've had no news of the villain since you left India?" he asked.

I shook my head. "None whatsoever."

He sighed reluctantly. "It may bring suspicion upon me to ask my superiors anything about the case, but I believe I have connections with the power and position to find what you may be looking for."

"Do you really?" I reached out for him immediately, clasping my hands around his upper arm. His uniform was starched and stiff beneath my fingers, but warm from his skin and the sun.

He tensed at my touch and smiled. "I believe so, but are you certain this is a path you want to tread? It seems to me the outcome will be bleak regardless. If they have found the man, you will be faced with the decision of whether you want to see him or not. If they have not found the man, you will continue on in fear that he may come for you again. I do not see a happy ending in either regard."

An invisible weight lifted off of me, and I wished for a moment Achilles Prideaux were around for me to boast of my success. I'd been in Simla for two days and had already made a useful connection. Just as I'd told Monsieur Prideaux time and time again in Morocco, I could take care of myself.

"Well, Lieutenant Collins, that is fine by me. I gave up

looking for happy endings a long time ago. Now, I search only for answers."

The Lieutenant inhaled, unhitching something in his chest like he was going to say something, but then thought better of it and tipped his head back to look at the sky. We lay on the checkered blanket in a heavy silence and watched as the clouds moved overhead.

6

M rs. Hutchins had been telling the truth when she'd told the Lieutenant she had no desire to be out of doors more than necessary. Over the next several days, she remained inside the bungalow, closed away in the darkest room of the house with a fan in one hand and a glass of water in the other.

"Going out again, Rose?" she called as I walked past the room where she was hiding out, my hat and a small bag tucked under my arm.

I reversed to look through the door. Her hair was frizzed at the ends, sticking out over her ears like she'd received a good shock, and her cheeks were perpetually flushed. If she looked this frazzled in Simla, I could only imagine how she must have been in Bombay.

"I'd like to get out and see more of the area," I said shortly, hoping not to be delayed too much. I had plans in the afternoon that I couldn't be late for.

"Arthur could accompany you if you are in need of someone to escort you," she said, raising her voice to be sure

Arthur would hear her from his permanent perch in the study next door.

"Oh no, I wouldn't dream of disturbing either of you," I said just as loudly. "You have been so kind to offer me a place to rest, and I would hate to inconvenience you. Besides, I am meeting friends this afternoon, so I have an escort."

This wasn't entirely true, but if things went as expected, I would be running into a few familiar faces at some point in the day.

"Will your group of friends include Lieutenant Graham Collins?" Mrs. Hutchins asked, pursing her lips in a tight smile. "Perhaps an old woman should not involve herself in affairs of the young, but you cannot deny me what little fun I have left. The man seemed sweet on you, Rose. He could scarcely pull his eyes away through all of lunch."

My face flushed. None of this was news to me, as I'd noticed the Lieutenant gave me special attention, but discussing the matter with Mrs. Hutchins felt too uncomfortable for words.

"I'm not sure if he will be there," I said, taking a step down the hallway, half-disappearing behind the door. "But I'm afraid I really must be going. Is there anything I can get you while I'm out?"

Mrs. Hutchins waved me away and went back to fanning herself. "No, no. Have a good time and don't spare a thought for this old woman. I'll be just fine here all day."

I didn't say so, but I had no intention of sparing Mrs. Hutchins a single thought for the rest of the day.

I hurried down the hallway and was almost to the front door when a hand shot out and seized the knob. I let out a yelp of surprise and stumbled back.

"Forgive me, Miss," Mr. Barlow said, his mouth drawn downwards in a frown. "I hope I did not frighten you."

Heart still racing, I shook my head and smiled. "No, I am too jumpy for my own good."

He bowed low and pulled the front door open for me. The entire exchange was strange. He was Mr. Hutchins' personal secretary, not a butler. Opening doors should not have been part of his job description. Perhaps, despite his relentless grim demeanor, he was just attempting to be friendly. In a house full of the Hutchins family, I was anxious for any reprieve I could find, and if that included becoming friends with the sunken-eyed man, then so be it.

"Thank you, Mr. Barlow." I returned his bow with a curtsy and hurried through the door and into the waiting car. I did not turn around to see, but I could feel him watching me until I finally heard the thud of the door close just as the car pulled away from the bungalow.

PEOPLE SWARMED AROUND ME, swirling like an angry sea, rising and falling in different directions with no warning. The chatter fell over me like rocks, deflecting off without sinking in. Despite the years I'd spend in India with the Beckinghams, I'd never familiarized myself with Hindi. There hadn't been a need. The British officials and their families spoke English, and I didn't converse with anyone else. Mr. Beckingham had known a little Hindi—enough to do business efficiently—but even he would have been lost in the bazaar. It was why we always travelled with our native driver or other servants. They acted as translators when necessary.

I needed a translator now. Or a guide. Someone to grab my hand and tell me to move, to go.

The locals swirled around me, but even without knowing their language, I could sense their annoyance. I was an obstacle in the flow of daily life, rooted to the spot where, eight months before, my life had changed forever.

I searched the road for some kind of scar or divot in the ground, similar to the one marring my left cheek, but there was nothing. No sign of the trauma, the horrors the site had endured.

When I looked across the road, I could see the traffic of that day. The crowds pressing in on the road like balloons filled with too much air, ready to burst and spill in front of the cars. I could see the stalls lining the roads, selling vibrantly-colored fabrics and foodstuffs. When I closed my eyes and inhaled, I could even smell the jasmine scent of Rose sitting next to me.

A shiver moved down my spine at the memory. A reminder of how that day ended. Of how that ordinary day, just like the one I was standing in the middle of, had been shaken. I glanced around at the crowd. Was anyone next to me there then, as well? Had our lives overlapped more than once?

I took a deep breath and looked across the marketplace. The shape of him came to me immediately. He was hunched forward, drab rags hanging from his small frame. A beggar, I'd thought at the time, offering him no more than a moment's notice. My eyes touched him for a second and then moved on without a second thought. Until, he lifted his face and his arm.

My eyes had been caught by the unusual item in his hand. The unnatural shape of it. I'd been so distracted that his face no longer mattered. My mind had wiped it from my memory completely in order to make more space for the thought that whoever he was, he had an explosive device in his hand. A bomb that was aimed at our car.

I blinked away tears and then wiped at them furiously. People were already staring at me as they passed, annoyed with my immobile stance, so crying would only draw more unwanted attention.

What was there to cry about, anyway? Tears wouldn't change the past. They wouldn't make me remember details that had been lost to time and trauma. I didn't have time for tears. And like I'd told Lieutenant Collins, I didn't hope to find a happy ending. I wanted to find answers.

LIEUTENANT COLLINS HAD BEEN RIGHT about the polo matches. Everyone attended. British soldiers, officials and their wives stood outside waiting to get in, standing on tip toes to gauge how much longer the wait would be. Excitement was palpable in the air, and I wondered Rose had never dragged me to a match with her. She resented the company of the other British families in India, calling them "pampered," as though she herself wasn't waited upon by servants and followed by a companion who was employed to keep her entertained—me. However, she loved knowing what everyone was doing. If she didn't know which activities they participated in, what would she make fun of them for later while we lay awake in her room? Rose had turned her nose up at the balls and dances and dinners, but I couldn't remember her ever mentioning the polo matches. So, I was surprised by the thrill moving through the crowd as we pressed through the gates.

"Miss Beckingham?"

I turned to see Miss Dayes standing before me in a bright green dress that fell to the middle of her shins, the fluttery sleeves tickling her elbows, and a matching hat that highlighted her red hair, which looked even brighter in full daylight.

"Miss Dayes," I said, leaning forward to embrace her in a quick hug. "So good to see you again."

"You must call me Jane and I shall call you Rose," she said. I had no opportunity to respond before she spoke again. "Are you alone?" she asked, brow furrowed as she looked around for any possible companions.

I nodded. "I am today."

"Then please, come with us," she said, waving for me to follow her and two other women who looked impatient to keep moving further up the path.

I opened my mouth to object, but sensing my intention, Jane Dayes crossed her arms. "Knowing you are here without friends, and I did nothing to stop it will ruin my entire day. Please, Rose. Come with us."

I sighed and smiled. "Well, I'd hate to ruin your entire day."

Sturdy wooden seating circled a low-cut grass field, and the stands were mostly full by the time I squeezed between rows to get to where Jane and her friends were sitting. Horses were pawing at the grass, their riders patting their sides and standing near their heads as though whispering in the horse's ears. Perhaps that was what they were doing. I didn't know enough about the game to be certain.

Suddenly, Jane gasped, and I looked to the field, wondering if the game had started. The horses and their riders were standing around just as they had been before. When I looked at her, she was whispering something to the brunette friend on her right. When she finished, she turned to me.

"*That*," she said, pointing at a pale, dark-haired woman in a black dress near the front of the stands, "is Elizabeth Hughes."

The girl had straight black hair that hung around her neck in a sleek kind of way. Between her hair and her black dress, she looked like she was in mourning. That was when a remembrance flickered in my mind.

"Is she related to—?"

Jane nodded. "Her father was Thomas Hughes, the man who hanged himself no more than a week ago."

I grimaced. Everyone around us was smiling and laughing and cheering. I couldn't imagine being surrounded by so many happy people so soon after such a public heartbreak. "A sporting event seems like a curious choice for her first foray back into society."

"I'd say so," Jane said, looking disgusted. "I'd never leave my house again if my father did such a thing. I'd leave the entire country to avoid ever speaking of it again. No one enjoys being reminded of such dreadful news. It is better to move where no one knows you and you can start fresh."

Suddenly remembering the dreadful news of my past, Jane looked at me nervously, perhaps waiting to see if I would remind her. Though I would have loved to be the person to remind someone like Jane Dayes to be more thoughtful of what she said and to whom, that was not the moment.

"Have you ever spoken to the woman before?" I asked. "Elizabeth Hughes, I mean."

She shook her head. "No, but I attended a dinner at the home of Mr. and Mrs. Wood last night, and their daughter Mary spoke to Elizabeth the day after her father's suicide.

The two have been friends since they were children, so Mary had gone to offer her condolences. And Elizabeth told Mary that she did not believe her father had committed suicide."

"What?" I asked, my gaze snapping back to study Jane as she spoke.

"I know," Jane said, eyes wide and disbelieving. "The man hanged himself in a public place. Who could dispute that? But she was overcome with grief at the time. I'm sure the shock has worn away, and she is being much more sensible now."

Elizabeth looked lost in the crowd. Her eyes were wide, but she kept her face low, turned towards the ground as though she wanted to hide. Shock was etched into every line of her young face. She looked broken, much as I had in the days after the attack on the Beckinghams. Why would she place herself in such a public space while she was clearly so distraught?

Thomas Hughes had been a General. Was that a position that would earn the attention of the same assassins I had encountered in Morocco and possibly in Simla eight months prior? It wasn't outside the realm of possibility. Perhaps, I needed to manufacture a run-in with Elizabeth Hughes.

A waving hand at the corner of my vision caught my attention, and I looked to my left to see a long arm in a dark soldier's uniform waving. It only took one guess to know who the arm belonged to.

"Lieutenant Collins," Jane Dayes shouted above the crowd, waving back. "Come up here."

Jane pushed on my shoulder, making space between us for the Lieutenant, who was currently shuffling towards us, squeezing between people who kept shooting him annoyed looks. Finally, he reached us and settled into the small space between us. My entire left side was pressed against his right, and he had to angle his chin in a funny way to look over at me.

"Miss Beckingham, always a pleasure," he said, smiling despite how squished he appeared. "I see you took my advice and decided to come to a polo match."

"I did," I said, offering him a wide, genuine smile in return. I'd followed his advice in the hope I would run into him at the sporting event, so I was pleased that my hunch had proven true. "I'm almost overwhelmed. Everyone seems to be having a grand time and the game hasn't even started yet."

"You can't live in India for any period of time without going to a polo match," the Lieutenant said. "So, it's good you came."

"And why is that? Does everyone know this rule about India?"

"India is the birthplace of modern polo," he said, waving his arms around in a grand gesture.

I smiled and returned my attention to the field.

The match started, an official blowing a whistle to begin the game. Lieutenant Collins pointed out things to me as the horses dashed around the field, the riders swinging mallets after a ball I could barely see in the glare from the sun, but his explanation did little to ease my confusion. I relegated myself to not understanding the rules and simply cheering when everyone around me did. It seemed to fool everyone because, after awhile, the Lieutenant stopped trying to explain the rules to me.

During a pause in the middle of the game, Jane moved down several rows to hug another friend of hers, leaving me and the Lieutenant mostly alone. I didn't think there would be a better time to bring up the real reason I'd come to the polo match at all, so I decided to dive right in.

"Have you uncovered any news about the bomber?" I asked quietly, pulling the Lieutenant down into the seat next to me, so we were both sitting.

He looked dazed by the sudden turn of the conversation, but then his face fell. "I found information, but if I'm honest, I hoped you would have forgotten about the idea entirely. I do not want to be the person to bring you news you don't want to hear. I want to be the person to make you smile."

My ears felt hot at his admission. Was the Lieutenant declaring his intentions?

"I promise to smile regardless of what you say," I said, curling my arm around his and patting the back of his hand.

He looked down at where our hands touched and then followed the curl of our arms up to my face. "The man believed to be responsible for the bombing was a local extremist."

"Was?" I asked, immediately picking up on his use of the past tense.

He nodded. "The man was captured and hanged shortly after the bombing. He has been dead for seven months."

I sagged in my seat, but quickly remembering my promise, I sat up and smiled. "Thank you for looking into the situation for me."

"You do not have to smile, Rose," he said. "I relieve you of your promise. I'm sure you are disappointed."

"You said the man was believed to be responsible. Are they not certain he committed the murders?" I asked. Surely, if the man had been killed, the note I'd found on the assassin in Tangier would have made mention of it. But then again, maybe not. I hadn't the faintest idea how international assassin rings operated. Would that be information that would be shared?

"They wouldn't have executed him if there had been any doubts," Lieutenant Collins said.

I remembered when my view of law enforcement had been so certain. When I believed the law to be infallible and criminals to be evil to the core. I couldn't decide whether I pitied or envied Lieutenant Collins for maintaining such an opinion.

"Where was he held prior to his execution?" I asked. "Would I be able to visit the location?"

The Lieutenant's eyes went wide. "You would not want to visit the prison. It is a nasty place, Rose. No place for a respectable young lady."

"I appreciate your concern for my wellbeing, Lieutenant, but I can handle more than most people would imagine."

"The men inside those walls are criminals," he said, whispering the word like it was a curse. "They are not the gentlemen you are accustomed to."

I thought of the encounters I'd had over the previous eight months. Of the liars and murderers I'd met and fought. Lieutenant Collins would faint if he knew the kind of men I'd talked to.

I smiled and pressed myself against his side, bumping my hip against his. "There is no man on earth as gentleman-like as you, Lieutenant. You may have an impossibly high standard."

His eyes shined with pleasure at the compliment.

"Would a gentleman like yourself know anyone who works in the prison?" I asked, squeezing his arm. "I know it may seem silly, but I'd like to see where he was kept. Any connection to him may offer the closure I've been seeking."

"I know someone," he said, looking at me from the

corner of his eye. "I cannot make any guarantees, but if you are truly insistent upon the idea, I could talk to him."

"I am insistent."

He gave me a grim smile. "How did I know you'd say that?"

"Because you are a very smart man, Lieutenant."

Once again, his eyes shined, and I achieved what I'd set out to.

7

"Miss Rose, please reconsider."

Lieutenant Collins was practically begging me to stay in the car.

"Your friend is inside waiting on us, Lieutenant. We shouldn't keep him waiting."

"He is not a friend of mine," he corrected quickly. "I know him from my early days in the service, but we have not spoken in many years until recently."

Lieutenant Collins had made it clear to me several times during the short drive from the bungalow where I was staying with the Hutchinses to the prison that the man allowing us into the prison was not a friend of his. He'd asked around, found someone with a connection in the prison, and realized he'd met the man on occasion in his youth. The guard was willing to allow us into the cell for only a few minutes as long as we stayed quiet and told no one.

"Well, there is a man inside waiting on us, and it would be rude not to show up."

He sighed and grumbled something under his breath

about being too nice—I suspected he was talking about his own propensity for doing things he did not agree with for my benefit—and walked around the car to open my door.

The guard met us at the gate. He was a wide man with a thick mustache, his stomach straining against the buttons of his brown uniform.

"Lieutenant," he said, winking at Lieutenant Collins. He turned and bowed to me. "And the curious lady."

"Miss Rose Beckingham," Lieutenant Collins responded, his tone sharp and commanding.

The guard straightened and tipped his head to me. "Miss Beckingham."

He led us down a wide, dim hallway with windows punched through the thick walls every twenty steps. Lieutenant Collins stayed close to me, hovering over me like he expected criminals to burst through the windows at any second.

The guard talked over his shoulder as we turned into a narrower hallway with a set of stone stairs that led deeper into the prison. "Civilians are not usually supposed to be inside the walls, especially women. So, I have to ask that you don't tell anyone who let you inside."

"Will we be in any trouble if someone catches us?" Lieutenant Collins asked.

The guard shook his head and then shrugged. "Not too much trouble. Just tell them who you are and why you are here, and they won't report you."

"They'll care that I'm a Lieutenant?"

"No," the guard responded, leaning around Lieutenant Collins to point directly at me. "They'll care that her family was killed in an attack less than a year ago. Everyone here hated the monster who threw the explosive. They'll understand why she wanted to come."

I blinked and swallowed a small lump in my throat. First, Lieutenant Collins had mentioned how much he'd wanted to offer me his condolences after the attack. And now a stranger working in the prison had mentioned widespread indignation at the crime. For so many months, I'd felt alone in my grief, but being back in Simla, I was faced regularly with people who had been touched by the attack in some way. The tragedy occurred in their town, so of course they cared. Of course, they remembered. For the first time in months, I didn't feel alone.

The cell was primitive. Dirt floor, stone walls, no windows. I could only pace five steps into the room before running into the far wall. Living in the space for more than a few hours would have sent me burrowing through the wall.

The man who had killed the Beckinghams deserved to be in a cell like this. He deserved far worse. But had they executed the right man? A large part of me wanted to believe they had because it was easy, because it allowed me to close that chapter of my life and move on. But I couldn't dispel the idea that the culprit was still walking free.

"Not much to see," Lieutenant Collins said, bending at the waist to poke his head through the short doorway.

"I only want to look around for a few minutes."

His eyes cast quickly around the room like he couldn't imagine what could be left to see, but then he backed into the hallway and stood up. The door was low enough that, because he was so tall, he could not see into the room without bending forward. It offered a semblance of privacy.

With nothing but a flickering lantern hanging from the wall next to the door, the edges of the room disappeared into shadow. I paced the short length of each wall, eyes trained on the floor for something. Anything. I had no idea what I was hoping to find or where whatever it was would be hidden. Had the idea to come here been foolish? The man who had stayed in the cell—probably one of hundreds over the years the prison had been operating—was dead. What kind of answers could I hope to find in a room no larger than my closet at the bungalow?

Then, I saw a light. Only a flicker, really. Just a glimmer on the far wall that connected the cell I was in to the next one. I moved towards it, hands outstretched, feeling the rough, crumbling wall until my fingers found a hole in the stone. I gasped.

"Rose? Is everything all right?"

"Fine," I said quickly, hoping the Lieutenant would stay outside for a few more minutes. I needed time to explore without being conscious of his eyes on me.

He sighed but stayed where he was in the hallway, pacing back and forth past the door.

I knelt down and put my eye level with the hole in the wall. Through the hole, which was no more than four fingers tall and two fingers wide, I could see into the adjoining cell. I ran my finger along the hole, trying to understand what it could have been used for, and felt a notch partway in. I reached into the groove and pulled out a small bundle of beads. Only when I turned around and held them up to the candlelight did I recognize them as prayer beads.

"Where did you find that?"

I jumped and clutched the beads to my chest. Lieutenant Collins was bent forward, looking at me through the door, his eyes narrowed.

"Sorry, I didn't mean to startle you," he said, stepping into the room and standing to his full height. The lantern was affixed to the wall at his shoulder-height, so harsh triangles of shadow covered his eyes and nose, turning his usually kind face menacing. "What is that?"

"A *mala*, I think," I said, turning the beads over in the palm of my hand, counting them. "I recognize them from the servants in the Be—" I barely stopped myself from saying *the Beckingham household*— "the Bombay house," I corrected. "They are Buddhist prayer beads."

The Lieutenant snorted and shrugged. "Even criminals have faith, I suppose."

"I suppose," I said, turning the beads in my hand again, running my fingers along the string. "Though, refraining from violence is the first precept of the Buddhist religion."

Lieutenant Collins blinked. "What are you saying?"

"I'm saying." I held the beads up in the air between us as though they would finish the sentence for me. "If the man convicted of the bombing was in fact a devout Buddhist, it seems unlikely he would have committed murder, no matter what views he might have held of the British Raj."

Lieutenant Collins pursed his lips. "Those beads could have belonged to anyone who stayed in this cell. We have no way to know—"

I rushed past Lieutenant Collins, ducking through the door and into the hallway. He scrambled to follow after me. "Rose, where are you—?"

A huff of air burst out of his chest when he ran into my back, as he was surprised by my sudden stop only a few feet away.

"What are you doing?"

I leaned down to look through the bars. The man inside the next cell looked like a frightened animal, huddled in the corner. His eyes were wide, reflecting the dim candlelight that made up his world. He stared at our legs, unable or unwilling to meet our eyes.

"Hello," I said, lifting a hand in greeting.

The man flinched at the sound of my voice.

"Do you know who these belong to?" I asked, holding up the beads.

"Rose, this is not what we discussed," Lieutenant Collins said, looking up and down the hallway for any sign of a guard. He was so visibly uncomfortable that a guard may have been a welcome sight to him.

The Indian prisoner looked at the beads, and though he said nothing, I caught recognition in his eyes. It was not the first time he'd seen them. When he glanced towards where I knew the hole in the wall was, my suspicion was only confirmed.

"Do you know Hindi?" I asked, turning to Lieutenant Collins.

His shoulders sagged. How many more favors could I ask him before he decided my friendship wasn't worth it? Hopefully one more, at least. "Passably. Only enough to get by."

"That's fine," I said, grabbing his arm and pulling him down with me, so we were both looking into the cell. "Ask him if he has seen these beads before."

The Lieutenant obliged—I noted his Hindi was considerably better than simply passable—and the prisoner glanced up, nodded, and then returned his eyes to the floor. "What else do you want me to say?"

"Ask him if they belonged to the man responsible for the bombing," I said.

Once again, the Lieutenant repeated my question in Hindi, but this time the man responded. A short answer, but still, it was progress.

"He says no," Lieutenant Collins said, standing up. "They aren't the beads of the bomber."

My heart sank as disappointment replaced the hope that

had been blooming in my chest. Perhaps, the attack had been a random happenstance. Maybe my desire to connect it to the international ring of assassins I'd been investigating with Monsieur Prideaux was just another way to distract myself. From what, I didn't know. But finding trouble had become a habit of mine, and maybe it was time to focus on something else.

Just as I was preparing to give up and leave, I heard a faint voice from inside the cell. Lieutenant Collins sighed and closed his eyes.

"What did he say?" I asked, grabbing his arm like a starving woman begging for a slice of bread.

The words came out of him reluctantly, mumbled through clenched teeth. "He said the beads belonged to the man *accused* of the bombing."

When I bent down, the man was closer to the cell bars than he had been before, the dim light illuminating the dirt caked around his feet and ankles from the floor. He looked wild.

"Do you not believe the man was guilty?" I asked. Lieutenant Collins repeated the question, his voice flat.

The prisoner shook his head and spoke. Lieutenant Collins interpreted. "The man I came to know was a devout Buddhist who protested his innocence every day until his death. He claimed he was falsely accused of the crime. His only crime was being nearby at the time of the explosion. He was a witness, but the police arrested him as the culprit. I believe his story."

"Neither of these men can be trusted," Lieutenant Collins said, shaking his head. "Of course, criminals will claim they are innocent."

I ignored him, giving him another question to translate.

"Did the condemned man ever say if he knew who had truly committed the crime?"

The answer came quickly. The Lieutenant said, "He saw the bomber, but the police would not accept his description of the man since they believed he was himself the culprit."

"What did he look like?" I was practically clinging to the bars, and Lieutenant Collins pulled me back, his hands on my shoulders.

The prisoner dragged a hand over his face, the skin around his eyes stretching, making his eye sockets look sunken in. He spoke and, again, the Lieutenant translated. "A skeleton devil."

I furrowed my brow and looked at Lieutenant Collins, waiting for him to translate the rest. "What else did he say?"

The Lieutenant shrugged. "That is it. He didn't say anything else."

"That's it? No hair color or eye color? Height, weight?"

Lieutenant Collins asked the man something, and the man shook his head. Apparently, skeleton devil was all I would get out of him. I didn't want to admit it, but the description was incredibly unhelpful.

"I can't imagine you found what you were looking for," Lieutenant Collins said as we left the prison, the guard who had let us in escorting us out. "What were you looking for anyway?"

Could I tell Lieutenant Collins that I was beginning to believe the man executed for the bombing had not been the true villain? What would he think of me then? Would he continue to help a woman he believed might be crazy? Probably not.

"I wasn't looking for anything specific," I lied. "Just more information about the man."

He nodded, holding open the door that led to the gated

area around the prison. The guard seemed relieved to have us outside the prison walls and ran ahead to unlock the gate.

"If I may be bold, Miss Rose," Lieutenant Collins said once we were back on the streets of Simla, the prison gate closed behind us. "I do not believe the man is worth any more of your time. The law has dealt with the likes of him, and you would be better served to live your life without another thought for him."

Lieutenant Collins' advice seemed sound. I could imagine myself fawning over him the way Miss Dayes did with Mr. Clarke. We would attend polo matches and hold hands during shows at the theater. It didn't matter what would come next—whether I'd stay in Simla to be with him or head back to London alone—because for once, I would be living for myself. I'd be enjoying the time I had while I had it, not focused on finding the next clue or speaking to the next witness.

The advice seemed sound, but that was because Lieutenant Collins didn't know what I knew.

The man responsible for the bombings was not a devout Buddhist who had suddenly turned radical. It didn't make sense, and in the preceding months, I'd learned that when things didn't fit together, it was because a key piece of the puzzle was missing. And I intended to find it.

8

Finding Elizabeth Hughes was easier than I would have imagined. Mrs. Hutchins actually held the answer. I found her in the sitting room—where she could be found most times of the day—with a fan still held firmly in her hand, her feet propped up on a tufted footrest.

"You asked Lieutenant Collins about a general the other day at lunch," I said, broaching the topic clumsily. I usually tried to be more subtle, but I didn't have time for subtlety.

She furrowed her brow and then her face smoothed, recognition replacing the confusion. "General Hughes? The man who committed suicide?"

I nodded and Mrs. Hutchins frowned. "Sad, sad story. I was shocked to hear of it while still in Bombay."

"But you said you did not know the man?"

"Correct," she said. "But of course, I've done my neighborly duty and sent along my condolences to his family. He has a daughter not much older than you, Rose. She must be beside herself with grief."

"Elizabeth Hughes," I said, acting as though Mrs.

Hutchins had jogged my memory. "I saw her in town yesterday, I believe. It was impossible at the time for me to speak with her, but perhaps I should send my condolences, as well."

"Yes, Elizabeth," she said, nodding slowly. Then, she smiled. "I sent a large bundle of white flowers bigger than me. They were extraordinary."

"They sound it. Do you still have her address handy? I'd like to stop and pay my respects, as well."

"There was a ribbon, as well," Mrs. Hutchins said, still thinking about the grandeur of her condolences. "A purple satin ribbon that she could reuse if she so wished. It would look wonderful on a dress."

"I'm sure she appreciated that," I said in a breath. "About the address. Do you remember it or know where I could find it?"

After describing to me the basket she had selected for the flowers and the most opportune time of day to send flowers so the recipient is most likely to be at home—mid-morning, after breakfast but before lunch—Mrs. Hutchins finally answered my question.

"Mr. Barlow will have that written down somewhere, I'm sure," she said with a dismissive wave. "He arranged the entire thing."

Mr. Barlow was drinking coffee in the dining room next to a day planner and the half-eaten breakfast left behind by his employer, Mr. Hutchins. I apologized for interrupting him and asked him for the woman's address.

"Are you familiar with Miss Hughes?" he asked, turning back several pages in his planner and marking a page with his finger.

I shook my head. "Not yet, but I thought I would reach out to her and try to make a connection."

Mr. Barlow lifted his chin, looking down at me over the length of his nose. "How very thoughtful of you."

I smiled at him. "We both lost loved ones in similar ways, so I thought it would be nice to offer emotional support."

"How so?" he asked, his lip curled back like he had just smelled something distasteful. "Your family was killed in a terrorist attack and her father killed himself. Forgive me, but I fail to see the similarities."

I leaned back, startled by the bluntness of the question. Mr. Barlow, who had been so quiet and reserved through the entirety of the train trip to the mountains, seemed oddly engaged in this conversation. It felt crazy to even consider, but Mr. Barlow looked suspicious, like he was trying to catch me in a lie or back me into a corner so I would make a confession of some kind. His usually sagging frame was rigid and tense. He looked like a hunting dog moments before it would dart into the trees after its prey. Did he know that I was investigating the circumstances of both Elizabeth's father's death and the Beckinghams'? Was it possible he could know I thought the man's suicide may have actually been a murder committed by the same hands that threw the bomb through the Beckingham's car window?

"Both deaths were very public," I explained, trying to keep my voice neutral. "Losing a loved one in that way is difficult, and I think I can offer her a small amount of comfort."

Mr. Barlow raised his eyebrows, stretching his thin, pale face long. Then, he did something I'd never seen before—he smiled. "I'm sure your friendship would be a comfort to her. I'm sorry you will meet under such poor circumstances."

He wrote the address down on a slip of paper and

handed it to me, turning his attention back to his coffee and the day's schedule as soon as the paper was in my hands. Without lingering, I turned and walked from the room, determined not to let paranoia isolate me. If I let myself get carried away, I'd find some deceit in every person I knew.

ELIZABETH LIVED in a tidy bungalow just outside the city. The nameplate next to the door named it as the home of General Thomas Hughes. As I knocked, I wondered if she would ever have the heart to change the nameplate.

When the door opened, I was surprised to see Elizabeth herself standing there in a black dress similar to the one I'd seen her in at the polo match. Her eyes were bloodshot, purple circles pressed under them from lack of sleep or exhaustion or both. She glanced up and down the street nervously before greeting me.

"How can I help you?"

"Hello, Elizabeth?" I said, suddenly doubting my plan. "We do not know one another, but I am—"

"Rose Beckingham," she said, taking a step back and appraising me.

I opened my mouth and then closed it, taken aback. "Yes, I am. We haven't met yet, but—"

"Your family was murdered in an attack committed by a *radical*," she said, placing special emphasis on the title.

"I'm sorry," I said, shaking my head, the vase of white peonies I'd been holding in front of me dropping to my side. "I don't understand what is happening. I came here to offer my condolences and—"

"Ask me about my father's death," she finished.

I sighed, frustrated with her interruptions and with the

lack of control I seemed to have in the situation. At the polo match, Elizabeth had looked the part of the grieving daughter, but now she looked half-deranged. Her eyes darted around like she was following the path of some zipping bug I could not see, and she spoke quickly and quietly as though someone would yank her back into the house at any moment and our conversation would be at an end.

Clearly, being honest would produce the best results.

"Yes, I'm here to ask you a few questions," I said.

She shook her head, her dark hair bouncing from the force. "You shouldn't be here, and we should not be talking."

I felt like I'd stepped into a dream. Or a nightmare, perhaps, would have been a more apt description. "What do you mean, Elizabeth?"

"Your family was murdered," she whispered, closing the front door so I could only see half of her face. "And so was my father. You may think that is a coincidence, but I do not. No good can come from you being here."

"You believe your father was murdered? People are saying he committed suicide."

"People say many things," she said, closing the door still more. I could only see one of her eyes and a stripe of cheek now. Her voice was muffled. "And people see many things. For whatever reason, our families were targeted, but we escaped. I do not intend to draw the ire of whoever is responsible."

"I only have a few questions," I said, resisting the urge to stick my fingers in the door and rip it open.

"Go to the White Tiger Club if you want to learn more about his death. No one there will know the truth, but I can't offer you any more than I already have."

With that, the door closed, and so did my opportunity to talk to Elizabeth Hughes.

9

I'd known Mr. Beckingham to frequent the White Tiger Club, and occasionally Mrs. Beckingham would tag along to "catch up with the girls" over a cocktail, but I had never been before, so I had little idea what to expect.

The club sat in the center of the town, not far from the headquarters of many departments of local and international government, allowing for officials to stop in for lunch during the day and take meetings there. Important looking men in suits stood around outside the front door as I walked up. Immediately, I worried my dark blue walking skirt and cream sweater were too informal for the kind of company I would find inside, but the doorman had already spotted me and was moving down the front steps to offer me his hand.

"Good afternoon. Your name, Miss?"

"Beckingham," I said, affecting as much importance to the name as I could. "Rose Beckingham."

If there was any recognition, the man did a fine job of hiding it. He nodded, assisted me up the three wide, flat stairs, and then left me on the top step to turn back to a wooden podium I hadn't noticed at first. On it was a pad of paper with a long list of names. His finger ran down the list and, upon reaching the bottom without seeing my name, back to the top. He glanced up at me for a second before going through the routine a second time.

"I'm sorry, Miss Beckingham, but I do not see your name. Do you have a membership?"

A membership? Of course, a club for government officials wouldn't let in just anyone. There would have to be a list of approved guests. I'd assumed the Beckingham name would be recognized and allowed in anywhere, but the heads of the house had been dead for eight months and their daughter—me—had moved to London. No one had been paying whatever exorbitant membership fees the club charged, so of course my name had been scrubbed from the list.

"Well, in fact," I started with no idea where the sentence would go from there. Could I just explain to the man who I was and why I didn't have an active membership? Even if he understood, he wouldn't risk losing his job for a random young woman. I couldn't tell the truth, and I wasn't prepared to lie. I was half-tempted to just sprint down the steps and disappear into the crowd moving past.

"She is with me," said a vaguely familiar baritone voice behind me.

I turned to see Lieutenant Collins, looking dashing as ever in his pressed uniform with his freshly-shaven face.

The Lieutenant leaned down to kiss me on the cheek, his hand pressed to my lower back. "Sorry to keep you waiting, my dear."

The doorman stood a little straighter. "Lieutenant Collins. Sorry, I didn't realize."

"That is because I didn't say." I offered the man a kind smile.

"I was supposed to meet you at home," the Lieutenant said, passing a tip to the doorman as we walked through the doors and into a dark wood and plant-covered lobby.

"My mistake, *dear*." I gave Lieutenant Collins a slight eyebrow raise as I repeated the endearment he'd used for me in front of the doorman. But now we were alone with no one close enough to overhear our conversation. "You did not need to save me."

"It looked like you were about to be removed from the premises. Do you not still have a membership?" he asked.

"Apparently not." I smiled and shrugged as though I couldn't be bothered with such details.

"Do you have plans here today?" he asked, glancing around the lobby to see if anyone was waiting for me. "Or will I have the pleasure of your company?"

"I wouldn't want to intrude on your plans, Lieutenant. I appreciate you getting me inside, but you do not need to rearrange your schedule for lunch with me." The sentiment was real, but I also didn't want to be tied down to the Lieutenant the way I had been in the prison. I wanted the freedom to talk to the staff and explore the rooms without suspicion.

"There is no schedule," he said, placing a hand on my lower back and leading me towards the dining room. "I came here with the hope of running into someone I could dine with, though I must admit I never imagined I would be so lucky as to run into you."

With no reason not to join Lieutenant Collins for lunch, I followed him into the dining room and to a table in the middle of the room where an Indian servant in native garb took our order. The Lieutenant ordered for us both and no sooner had the serving man walked through the swinging door into the kitchen, than another man approached the table.

"Major McKinley." Lieutenant Collins beamed and stood up to shake the man's hand. "I'm surprised to see you."

The Major, a beast of a man with bright red hair, rolled his eyes. "Please tell me you didn't expect me to mourn at home the way everyone else here clearly expected."

He had a thick Scottish accent and a booming voice that drew the attention of all the guests surrounding our table.

A blank expression passed over Lieutenant Collins' face. "I'm sorry, I don't know—"

Major McKinley pulled out a chair and dropped down into it so forcefully I thought the legs would snap. "The entire staff here and most of the guests look at me like I'm the one who hanged myself from the library rafters. So, I saw a dead body, who cares? Who in the military hasn't? I've seen scenes far more gruesome than a purple face."

I adjusted my posture in my seat and Lieutenant Collins spared a quick glance in my direction to see how I was reacting to the Major's gruff demeanor. I winked at him, and he seemed to relax, turning back to our new lunch guest. I had been shocked by the Major's words not because they were crude, but because he had just admitted to being the man who found Thomas Hughes' body in the club's library. Just as Lieutenant Collins claimed he couldn't imagine getting so lucky as to run into me at the club, I never would have imagined I'd be lucky enough to have a personal connection to the man who found the deceased man's body.

"I'm sure everyone wants to be sensitive to the situation," Lieutenant Collins said in a clear attempt to deescalate the conversation.

The Major barked. "I do not need sensitivity. I didn't

even know Thomas Hughes. We Scots are a hardy people and don't waste time crying over spilled milk, as the saying goes."

"Surely suicide is more important than a glass of spilled milk," I said, inserting myself into the conversation. I leaned across the table and offered my downturned fingers to the Major. "Rose Beckingham."

He raised a red eyebrow at me and then smiled as he accepted my hand, shaking it twice before letting go. "I'm not so mean as to say the death isn't a tragedy, but I'm not going to avoid the premises because of it."

"And we are glad you didn't," Lieutenant Collins said. "Avoid the premises, that is. We are happy to have you for lunch. Are you going to eat?"

The Scot lifted his upper lip. "You can eat the food here? I can't stomach it. All the local spices make me sick. I ate at home before I came but thank you for the invitation." He turned to me. "And how did you come to find yourself in the company of our shared friend Lieutenant Collins. Is he courting you?"

Words burst out of Graham, evidently before his lips were prepared for them, resulting in a kind of strangled, panicky sound. "No, no. Miss Beckingham and I are new friends. We ran into one another out front by pure happenstance."

Major McKinley angled one eyebrow up and looked at me with a new kind of appreciation that made me less interested in a conversation with him.

"I assume you two know each other through the service?" I asked.

Both men nodded. "What has it been now?" the Major asked. "Six years?"

The Lieutenant smiled. "That sounds about right."

"And not a woman in his life that entire time," Major McKinley play whispered, elbowing the red-faced Lieutenant in the side. "So, imagine my shock when I saw him sitting here with the prettiest woman in the room."

There was nothing I hated more than a forced compliment, especially one at the expense of another. Still, I needed to speak to Major McKinley about what he'd seen in the library the day General Hughes allegedly hung himself, so I couldn't afford to anger him. I went for the subtle approach.

"I'm sure Lieutenant Collins has always had his pick of the women. I appreciate a man who can set aside frivolous relationships in the name of advancing his career first. It is admirable."

Lieutenant Collins was once again red-faced, though I suspected it was for a much different reason now. He was too kind and had granted me so many favors that I couldn't sit by and watch him be embarrassed by a man who was meant to be his friend.

"It can't be helped," Major McKinley carried on, as though I hadn't spoken. "The women here are either the silly daughters of low level officials or native girls, neither of which are worth anything to a man of high standing." He looked at me with his eyes narrowed. "Present company excluded, I'm sure."

At first, I'd believed the Major's harsh opinion of General Hughes' death could have been because of a personal dispute between the two, but I was beginning to realize the General had a negative view of most people. The only kind word I'd heard him say had been about the hardiness of his own countrymen, though I suspected he could muster up a few harsh words for them, too, if the conversation required it.

Suddenly, he flung his hand in the air and waved it around, flagging down a passing male server who kept his eyes trained on the carpet as he approached, a nervous look in his eyes. "Am I not a paying member? Is anyone here going to offer me a drink?"

He ordered a scotch, and I hoped the Major was not an angry drunk. If so, the club had better be cleared out or *everyone* would be hanging from the rafters.

After the server left, the Major commented, "I can hardly understand a word these people say." He pulled out a cigar box from the inside pocket of his jacket and weighed a thick cigar between his fingers. "Can I borrow your cutter, Lieutenant?"

Lieutenant Collins fished a metal cigar cutter from his own inside pocket and handed it to Major McKinley. The Major snipped off the end of his cigar and ran it under his nose, inhaling loudly. "I misplaced mine a week or two ago and haven't been bothered enough to buy a new one yet. I keep assuming it will turn up eventually."

"Things like that usually do," I said.

The two men talked about shared friends and the various events they were looking forward to or dreading over the coming week, and I did my best to stay engaged, but my attention was mostly focused on finding a way to get the Major alone. I needed to talk to him about the General's death without Lieutenant Collins around. The Lieutenant had been willing enough to grant me a few favors and put himself in uncomfortable positions to help me grieve the loss of my family, but I couldn't imagine he would show the same understanding towards my interest in the death of one of his peers whom I hadn't known in the slightest. Everyone had their limits.

Our food arrived, and after snapping at the Indian server

for another drink and turning up his nose at the smell of our meal, Major McKinley leaned back in his chair, crossed his legs, and puffed on his cigar as if he was in a smoking room rather than the dining room. I could tell Lieutenant Collins, always the gentleman, found Major McKinley to be an unwanted addition to our lunch party, but his unfailing manners made it impossible for him to say so. If I hadn't wanted to speak with the Major, Graham's politeness would have been frustrating, but as it was, it worked to my benefit.

"The menu listed honey roasted carrots as a side dish, did it not?" I asked, searching through the food on my plate with my fork, as if looking for the nonexistent carrots.

Lieutenant Collins twisted his lips to one side and furrowed his brows. "I don't remember seeing roasted carrots listed, but my memory is not the greatest. Especially when it comes to vegetables."

I laughed and touched his shoulder. "A strong man like yourself must eat his vegetables."

"Not unless forced," he said laughing, his cheeks pink.

"Then I will have to force you," I said, sliding my chair away from the table. "Let me ask someone about the discrepancy with the carrots and see if it can be remedied."

Before I could even lift myself out of my chair, Lieutenant Collins did just as I'd expected. He stood up and pushed my chair back under the table. "Allow me, Rose."

I gave him a warm smile over my shoulder, admiring the clean-cut beauty of his face as he turned and walked towards the swinging kitchen doors. But not allowing myself to be distracted, as soon as the Lieutenant was out of hearing range, I turned my attention back to the Major.

"I gathered by our conversation upon your arrival that you are the person who found General Hughes." The Major didn't strike me as the kind of man who needed to be eased into a difficult line of questioning. He would have a greater respect for me if I showed no reservations.

Major McKinley sat up straighter at the sound of my voice but maintained his cross-legged position with his cigar balanced between his thumb and forefinger. "You gathered correctly."

"I also gathered you may not have cared for the man," I continued.

The Major shook his head. "No, that isn't it. I hardly knew him, if we are being honest. We passed in the hallways and I would see him across the dining room on occasion, but we had never spoken before, so I had no reason not to like him."

"Sorry for my assumption, but the way you discussed his death made me believe the two of you may have had a history."

He lifted his lips in a small smile and tilted his head to the side, studying me. "You were bothered by my comparison between the General's death and spilled milk."

"Not bothered," I said, cutting a piece of food and chewing slowly. "Just surprised. Most people would have been more disturbed by the sight of a dead body."

"Like I said, I've seen much worse during my time as a soldier."

"But the White Tiger Club is far from a battlefield," I said, gesturing to the room around us with its crystal chandeliers and busy waitstaff. "I am not afraid of deer, but I'd scream if I saw one in my own sitting room."

"Fair enough." The Major smiled at my comparison and then leaned forward until his cigar was hovering over the Lieutenant's dinner plate. "To be honest, I did not see much of the scene. I had never even been in the library before that day, so it is a complete coincidence that I'm the person who found General Hughes at all. I opened the door to see what the room was used for and saw a man suspended in mid-air."

"What did you do then?" I asked.

"Is this an inquisition? Do I need to bring the Lieutenant back to defend me?" he asked playfully, though I sensed his defensiveness.

"Only if you feel you need defending."

"I left," he said with a loud sigh, as though it should have been obvious. "I know many people want to think I left because I was afraid or startled, but I left to avoid disturbing the scene and because it was obvious to me that the General was dead. I needed to alert the staff to the situation and get the authorities to the club as soon as possible."

"After seeing a man hanging from the rafters, you didn't feel any desire to attempt to cut him down while yelling for help?" I asked.

The Major narrowed his eyes. "What many people who have never been faced with the realities of life and death don't understand is that human nature is animalistic. When under duress, our bodies are not operating on a moral code. When I saw General Hughes puffy-faced and hanging from the ceiling, I was not thinking about him or his wellbeing, I was thinking about my own safety. Many would say that is cruel, but anyone who says that has never been in a similar situation. My desire was to get away from whatever threat may have caused the General to end up dead, and I would suggest anyone else in a similar situation do the same thing. Run away from the danger and stay away." He paused for a moment, maintaining steady eye contact until I blinked and looked away. Then, he leaned back in his chair and laughed. "It is why you will never find me in another library."

Did Major McKinley know who I was? Everyone else I'd

encountered in Simla had recognized my name, and he did not seem like someone who was out of touch with local events. So, did he know I had been in a life or death situation less than a year before? Did he really think it necessary to explain to me how the body responded to stress?

Or, was this a warning?

Run away from danger and stay away.

Major McKinley was the only Scottish man I'd met in Simla. Did that make him more or less suspicious? A trained assassin would want to blend in. He wouldn't disguise himself as a loud Scottish Major. Or would he?

My mind was spinning with possibilities I hadn't even been considering moments before, and I felt entirely out of my depth. Thankfully, or perhaps not so—I was quite frazzled in the moment—Lieutenant Collins returned.

"The carrot debacle has been handled." He tossed his cloth napkin over his lap and sighed. "They are making some right now. Apparently, they aren't on the menu, but with a little persuasion, they agreed to prepare some special."

"You didn't have to go to such trouble," I said, papering on a thin smile.

Lieutenant Collins smiled at me and patted my hand with his. "When are you going to realize you are no trouble to me, Rose?"

Major McKinley caught my eye, one of his fiery eyebrows raised in suspicion, letting me know he didn't have the same warm opinion of me as the Lieutenant. To him, I looked like trouble.

MAJOR MCKINLEY LEFT before we finished our meal and

Lieutenant Collins had a meeting right after lunch, so I would finally be alone inside the club. However, it was all I could do to force the Lieutenant to leave and allow me to find my own way home.

"I have been exploring town all morning," I insisted, pushing him towards the doors that led to the entrance hall. "I am perfectly capable of escorting myself around."

He looked towards the doors and back to me, unsure. "I feel horrible deserting you this way."

"You can't desert me if we didn't have any plans to begin with. This lunch was just a happy circumstance, remember?"

Had he not been in serious danger of being late, I wasn't sure I would have ever gotten rid of him. But finally, he pressed a quick kiss to my cheek, thanked me for my company, and flew through the doors without looking back. I hesitated in the entrance hall for a moment, making sure no one was paying any serious attention to me, and then turned and walked down the hallway marked "members only."

Wood paneling came halfway up the walls, the top half covered in a dark blue and yellow floral pattern that, when looked at quickly, resembled a thousand sets of eyes watching me. The illusion could have been because I was trespassing, but regardless, I felt like I was being spied upon.

A rectangular plaque stuck out above a set of double doors with the word 'Library' printed on it in gold. In the retelling of General Hughes' death, I'd imagined the library to be a central room in the club with several doors going in and out to other spaces, but in reality, it was quite secluded. Not the "public space" Miss Dayes had made it out to be. In fact, aside from faint voices coming underneath a door near the mouth of the hallway, I had not seen or heard another human since I'd left the entrance hall.

I stood in front of the solid wooden doors, wondering whether I should knock or walk right in. The latter option seemed the most authoritative, but it also lent itself to the possibility that I would storm in on a private meeting or, heaven forbid the same situation occur twice, a man preparing to commit suicide. Knocking, however, seemed meek, and I didn't want anyone to doubt my presence here more than necessary. So, steeling myself with a few deep breaths, I pushed the doors open and walked in as though I knew exactly where I was going.

Several paces in, I realized the room was empty. Shelves lined the walls and stretched up to the high ceilings, and a number of seating areas were arranged throughout the room—one in the center with a leather couch and sofas, one in the far corner with a wooden table and four wooden chairs, and then another just to the right of the door with three plush armchairs each with their own reading lamp. Every seat was empty. I closed the doors behind me and moved in slowly.

I half-expected a portion of the room to be roped off to stop people from walking through the location where, less than a week ago, a man had died, but there was nothing. The room seemed quiet, peaceful. Then, I looked up slowly, almost reluctantly, not wanting to look at the rafter where Thomas Hughes had hung, but I had to.

It was a thick wooden beam that ran the entire length of the room. It looked to be quite wide, plenty sturdy enough to hold the weight of a grown man, even one as large as Major McKinley. The amount of space between the beam and the arched ceiling also left plenty of room for a rope to be thrown from the floor, looped over the beam, and fall down on the other side. In terms of death by hanging, the library in the White Tiger Club almost seemed to be made for it. So, that much of the story checked out.

I walked the edges of the room, glancing up at the rafter every few steps, trying to discover what there was to see. What did Elizabeth Hughes know that led her to believe her father hadn't committed suicide? Was it simply that she didn't believe him capable or was there something else? I desperately wished I could talk with her. Our conversation had been frustratingly brief, and I highly suspected it would never happen again. Whether her paranoia was justified or not, it would keep her quiet.

After circling the room twice, I finally moved to the leather couch in the center of the room and sat down, letting myself sink into the cushion. Was I paranoid? The fact that I was asking the question made me believe I wasn't, but I couldn't be certain. Had the man in that prison cell with the Buddhist prayer beads been the same man I'd seen throwing the bomb in the marketplace? Was I looking for trouble where there wasn't any, purely because I could not accept that the Beckinghams had been killed in a random attack? Was Thomas Hughes simply a disturbed man who had sought relief in the only way he knew how? Because truthfully, I couldn't understand how the two cases could be connected. It had been observed before that Elizabeth and I were in similar situations after losing our family members in such public ways, but was there more to it than that? Had our family members been taken by the same hand or was I looking for connections where there were none to be found?

With no evidence and nothing solidly tying the case of the Beckinghams to Thomas Hughes, I was beginning to doubt my theory. In fact, I was beginning to doubt myself. For the first time since leaving him in Tangier, I wished

Achilles Prideaux were with me. He had the uncanny ability to shed light on situations, allowing me to see things more clearly, and I felt like I was sitting in the dark. I needed light desperately.

I studied the rafter again, hoping to see a secret note or symbol scrolled on the underside of the wood, but there was nothing. So, I sighed and moved to stand up. As I did, the heel of my shoe caught something just under the lip of the sofa, and I heard a metallic clatter across the hardwood floor.

The back of the sofa was open to the rest of the room, so I walked around the piece of furniture and knelt down behind it, holding the back of my skirt against my legs. Along with a great deal of dust, I noticed a palm-sized silver tool underneath the sofa. Careful to avoid dusting the floor with the sleeve of my cardigan, I reached out blindly until I felt the cool metal in my hand. When I stood up, I held it to the light and recognized it immediately as a cigar cutter, a small tool I'd seen Mr. Beckingham use for its intended purpose and also fiddle with often when he and Mrs. Beckingham were having a disagreement.

Assuming a man in the club had simply dropped the cutter, I began walking around the couch to set it on the glass-topped coffee table. But as I went to set it down, my thumb brushed across the back, and I noticed indentations in the metal. *Major Gordon McKinley.*

Bits of our lunch conversation came back to me, things that had seemed so unimportant, I'd hardly paid any attention. Now, I went back through every word, combing them for clues.

Major McKinley had asked to borrow Lieutenant Collins' cigar cutter.

"I misplaced mine a week or two ago and haven't been both-

ered enough to buy a new one yet. I keep assuming it will turn up eventually."

That alone meant nothing. The Major had admitted he'd misplaced his cigar cutter, and I'd found it, thus proving his story. The problem was that he'd misplaced it at least one week ago, by his own admission, which was prior to General Hughes' death. How could that be possible if he had never been in the library before the day he found the General's body hanging from the ceiling?

"I had never even been in the library before that day, so it is a complete coincidence that I'm the person who found General Hughes at all. I opened the door to see what the room was used for and saw a man suspended in mid-air."

Why would the Major lie about something as trivial as having been in the library? Was it a simple exaggeration in the name of story-telling? An understandable desire to distance himself from the trauma of the day he'd found the body? Or, had he lied in an attempt to disguise the truth that he had killed the General?

The door to the library opened, and I startled, dropping the cigar cutter and sending it sliding across the floor once again. It only stopped when it collided with the feet of a young Indian girl carrying a broom and dust pan. She looked just as shocked to see me as I'd been to see her.

"I am sorry. I did not know anyone was in here," she said in perfect English, grabbing the cigar cutter and walking it over to me, her face turned towards the floor.

"That's all right. Actually, you can keep it," I said, gesturing to the cigar cutter in her hand. "It doesn't belong to me. I just found it beneath the sofa. I think it is the property of Major McKinley."

Her eyes widened at his name, confirming that the

Major had either terrorized her the same way he had the server over lunch, or his rude reputation had preceded him.

"Do you mind returning it to him?" I asked.

The girl pressed her lips together tightly and shook her head.

"If it is a problem, I'm happy to do it myself," I said, holding out my hand. "I know he can be an intimidating man."

She glanced around the room to confirm we were alone, and then her shoulders sagged, her relief palpable. "He can be, yes."

I smiled and took the item from her. She appeared noticeably happier to be rid of the task. "Has Major McKinley belonged to the club for a long time?"

She shook her head. "He is a new member. Just within the last year."

Within the last year. When the bombing and the "suicide" of General Hughes had occurred. It could easily be a coincidence, but I filed the information away in my head for later.

"And does he frequent the library often?" The question was specific, and I didn't want her to become suspicious. "It is just that I cannot imagine him opening a book. I daresay I'd pay someone for the privilege of seeing him reading."

Her eyes widened from the scandal of my words, but I noticed her trying not to smile. "I've never seen him in the library before, but then, I do my best to avoid him. The staff use codes to alert one another where he is in the club."

"That is understandable," I said with a smile. Then, I leaned in, lowering my voice. "I hope I'm not making you uncomfortable, but I wonder if you were working here the day General Thomas Hughes was found."

Her eyes flicked towards the rafters of their own volition and she swallowed. "I was."

"Did you see anything unusual?"

The girl bit her lower lip and looked up at me from beneath long lashes, her brown eyes wide and nervous. She couldn't have been much older than seventeen. Just a child.

"I would never say a word," I said, holding my finger to my lips.

She mulled it over for another few seconds and then leaned in quickly. "I was leaving the smoke room, which is next door to the library, only ten minutes before the body was found, and I saw a man walking down the hallway."

"Is that unusual?" I asked, failing to see the importance of this detail.

She sighed, her shoulders sagging. "I was asked whether I had seen anything unusual that day since I had been working in the area, and I told everyone I had not because I did not think I could convey the importance of what I had seen."

"I wasn't trying to discredit your observation. Please, continue. Tell me what you saw."

The girl fidgeted with the broom, running her fingers nervously up and down the handle. "I did not see which room he came out of, but the feeling I had when he turned around and looked at me. It felt like looking into the eyes of the devil."

"The devil?" I asked.

She nodded and let her head fall forward. "I did not want to say anything and get anyone in trouble, especially since the death was later ruled a suicide, but the man I saw had done something evil, Miss Beckingham."

I startled. "How do you know my name?"

Shock and then embarrassment crossed her face, pinking the bridge of her smooth nose. "I'm sorry."

I laughed. "Do not apologize. I'm only curious how you have come to know my name before I am aware of yours?"

"My name is Rashi," she said, bowing her head forward. "My best friend is a servant girl in the Hutchins' home, and she told me you were staying there."

"Pleasure to meet you, Rashi. I hope your friend had nice things to say." Internally, I cringed. Did servants speak of me the way they did Major McKinley? Was I feared or hated for uncivil behavior?

"Oh, yes," she said, almost lunging forward to correct me. "Jalini says you are incredibly kind and clean up after yourself, which is better than other wealthy women."

The girl clamped a hand over her mouth, and I could tell by the glassiness in her eyes that she was seconds away from crying, fearing she had said too much. Our interaction was taking years off of her life, so for her own sake, I decided to cut it short.

"I'm glad Jalini thinks so," I said, smiling and reaching out to pat her arm. "I will be sure to tell her I met you when I see her next."

She shook her head. "I almost wish you would not. I made a fool of myself, I am sure."

"Certainly not. Thank you for enduring my questions."

I moved around Rashi and towards the doors but was stopped by the feeling of her hand on my arm. "Miss Beckingham?"

"Yes?" I turned back to her, a friendly smile on my face, one that fell as soon as I saw the fear in the girl's eyes. "What is it, Rashi?"

"The man I saw that day, he may not have had anything to do with General Hughes, but his intentions are dark," she said, her voice so unnaturally low it sent shivers down my spine. "I know a demon when I see him, and he was one. A ghoul walking among us. Please be careful, Miss."

Then, she removed her hand from my shoulder, turned around, and began sweeping the floors.

10

Mrs. Hutchins was lying down for an afternoon nap when I returned to the bungalow, and Mr. Hutchins was closed away in his study. I could not understand why either of them had bothered to leave Bombay. They rarely left the house, and aside from the guests they'd had over for lunch the first full day after our arrival, I hadn't seen them welcome any visitors or leave for a single event since we'd arrived. Somehow, I'd found myself staying with two of the least social people in all of Simla, and as much as I didn't want to talk to the Hutchins more than necessary, it made for a rather boring day. So, I went for a walk around the grounds.

The sky was a clear blue that looked more like a painting of the sky rather than the real thing. Birds sang in the trees and a soft breeze rolled down from higher up the mountain, bringing with it the fresh smell of clouds and pine trees. It was a lovely day, marred only by the dark nature of my thoughts.

Rashi had described the man she'd seen that day as a ghoul, a demon. She knew who Major McKinley was and what he looked like, so if he had been the one coming from the library, she would have known it. Though, she couldn't even be sure the demon-like man had come from the library. He could have simply been walking down the hallway past the library. Wrong place at the wrong time.

However, another thought plagued me. The man condemned for the Beckingham bombing had described the true assailant as a skeleton devil. Two people had described a man as being demonic. Was that a coincidence? Perhaps, a flair for the dramatic in both witnesses? Or, did it mean something?

Though I could not recall the face of the man who threw the bomb that so altered my future, I could clearly see the rags he'd worn. They were thick, almost like blankets draped across his shoulders, hanging down in tatters. The garments could have been hiding any-sized frame beneath them. From a man the size of Major Mckinley, huddled beneath the clothing, to someone not much larger than myself stretching to their full height. My recollections did little to make the picture of the attacker any more clear, and unfortunately, the two sightings of a demon man did not help, either.

I heard footsteps on the path and looked up to see Mr. Barlow coming around a bend in the trees. He wore his usual black suit and oxfords and looked incredibly out of place in the middle of a forest path. Though, Mr. Barlow looked out of place in most settings. His hollowed cheekbones, large eye sockets, and pale skin gave him the appearance of raw dough stretched over an unbaked pie, the dough sinking into the hollow places.

"Good afternoon, Mr. Barlow."

The man looked up without surprise, his eyes landing on me, sending a shiver down my spine despite the warm day. He tipped his head, holding onto the brim of his hat. "Miss Beckingham."

"Lovely day," I offered, hoping to make the time spent walking towards one another slightly more bearable with light conversation.

He nodded. "Did you meet with Miss Hughes today?"

"Yes, I did." I stumbled over the words, surprised by his sudden change of conversation.

"How is she faring?"

I didn't know how much to tell Mr. Barlow. First, I hardly knew the man myself. Second, aside from sending along Mrs. Hutchins' condolences, he did not know Elizabeth, either. It seemed disrespectful to tell him the woman might be having an attack of paranoia, especially since her paranoia could very well be justified.

"As one could expect," I said simply. Then, I lied. "She was grateful for my visit. Thank you for giving me her information."

Mr. Barlow tipped his head again. This time, because of the light coming through the trees on our particular stretch of the path, the sunlight cut across his face, leaving dark shadows beneath his eyes, and a thought appeared in my head without warning.

Skeleton devil.

I blinked the thought away, and by the time I refocused my eyes on his face, the shadow had passed and Mr. Barlow looked thin and pale as always. Unusual, but not malicious.

"Of course," he said. "You two have both suffered greatly, and I'm glad I could be the one to connect you."

Was it a trick of the light, or was he smiling? His thin, flat lips appeared to be turning up at the corners. Before I could further examine the expression or think of anything to say, we were passing one another, Mr. Barlow stepping to the far edge of the path to allow me room to walk, and then he was gone. I turned and watched his narrow frame round the corner and disappear into the trees.

As soon as the man was out of my sight, I scolded myself for being so susceptible to suggestion. Yes, Mr. Barlow better fit the description of a skeleton than the bulky Major McKinley, but thinness was no reason to suspect a man of murder. Besides, Rashi had spoken more to the look of the man's eyes than his physical description. Perhaps, the man I'd spoken to at the prison had misunderstood his prison mate's description of who he believed to be the true bomber. Maybe "skeleton devil" referred to something other than physical appearance. Perhaps, and more and more I was beginning to think this the more likely scenario, the description simply meant that the man represented death.

My shoulders rose to protect my neck as if from a winter chill. If the man really did represent death, then I would be wise to listen to Rashi's warning. I'd have to be more careful moving forward in my investigation.

BACK INSIDE THE BUNGALOW, I set out to find Rashi's friend Jalini for no other reason than I needed something to do. Plus, it would be nice to have a friend inside the bungalow. So, I walked through the dining room and into the kitchen.

The room was cramped with only a single window looking out over the backyard and offering any kind of daylight. I'd spent so long enjoying the life of a wealthy official's daughter that I'd almost forgotten what it felt like to spend my days in the servant's quarters.

There were two women chopping herbs and preparing what was sure to be dinner for the evening. They both looked up as I came in, tipped their heads in greeting, and then went back to their work. I could feel in the air that they had just been talking, but had fallen silent on my account.

"I hope I'm not interrupting," I said.

"Of course, not," one of the women said. She was an English woman, a servant brought over from London, probably just for the summer to help in the rented bungalow. "You are welcome to go wherever you'd like, Miss Beckingham."

I smiled at her and her helper, an Indian girl with long black hair twisted into a bun at the base of her neck and a dark freckle on her chin. "And you two are free to continue your conversation. Please, don't let me interrupt. I'm desperate for something to do. This bungalow is full of dreadfully boring people."

They both smiled, delighted with my honesty.

"Don't you both think so?" I asked. "Or are most homes you work in this quiet?"

The Indian girl shook her head. "I have never worked in such an uneventful home. It makes the work easier, but I would almost rather have a large feast to prepare."

"I'm tired of making soup," the English woman said. "It is all the Hutchins' seem to want to eat. It takes almost no time at all, and then we are left to dust the same rooms that no one has used all day."

"And here I am complaining of boredom to you," I said, laughing and shaking my head. "You both have it worse than me. I can leave whenever I'd like. I've actually just come from the White Tiger Club. Have you heard of it?"

Both women nodded.

"I met a girl there. Her name was Rashi," I said, looking carefully at the Indian servant's face. Obvious recognition lit up her eyes. "She told me I might find a Jalini working in my bungalow."

The English servant elbowed her friend. "This is Jalini right here."

Jalini gave me a shy smile, but I could tell she was delighted I knew her name.

"She told me all of your secrets," I said, raising an eyebrow.

Jalini's smile fell away, replaced by mild horror. I laughed. "I was prepared to tease you, but I wouldn't dare break up a friendship over a joke. No, Rashi told me only the nicest things. So nice that I wanted to come back and meet you immediately."

Jalini opened her mouth to say something but was cut off by the sound of footsteps on the stairs followed by Mrs. Hutchins' shrill shout. "Hannah!"

The English servant stood up straight, dropped her knife on the table, bowed to me, and rushed out of the room.

"I understand she is Hannah, then?" I asked, hitching my thumb over my shoulder.

"Yes, Miss," Jalini said. She continued working, keeping her head low.

"While you have been subjected to endless boredom here, Rashi had nothing but excitement down at the White Tiger Club. If you count the death of a guest as excitement," I said.

"It was horrible news," Jalini said. "Rashi was very distraught by all of it. She did not see the dead man, but the whole event left her shaken."

"As it would anyone," I said. "Being so close to death is an uncomfortable experience. Though, Rashi also mentioned to me that she saw a man near the scene of the death that gave her an uneasy feeling. Did she mention that to you?"

Jalini shifted her feet uncomfortably.

"I do not wish to pry on information shared between friends, so you do not have to tell me if you don't wish."

"It is not that I do not want to tell you," she said. "It is that I do not want to tell anyone."

I leaned forward, unable to help myself. This conversation was taking an interesting turn I had not at all expected. If anything, I'd simply hoped for a better description of the man Rashi had seen, but it appeared as though Jalini may have had information of her own. "Tell anyone what?"

"It is superstition," she said quietly, shaking her head as though scolding herself for mentioning it at all. "A local tale whispered amongst silly girls in search of excitement."

"Then there is no reason you shouldn't tell me. I am in search of excitement," I said, gesturing to the fact that I was standing in the kitchen talking to the servants.

Jalini sighed, set down her knife, and turned to me. "For the last year or so, villagers living on the western outskirts of the city have claimed to see smoke and movement coming from an uninhabited part of the forest. At first, they believed it to be nothing more than a stranger, someone passing through, but then people began to see a ghost moving between the trees."

"A ghost?" I asked, the disappointment clear in my voice. It sounded like it really was a local folktale.

"A ghost," she repeated, shrugging. "Others call him a skeleton. A demon."

Skeleton. Demon. I felt the hair on the back of my neck rise.

"People have gone to investigate, and someone claims to have found a hut in the trees that the man uses when he is in the area, but no one has ever seen him. Not up close, anyway."

"What does this have to do with what Rashi saw?"

"She believes she saw this man the day General Hughes died," Jalini said.

"And do you believe her?"

"I try not to think about it. I do not wish to cause grief to anyone."

I tilted my head to the side, trying to draw her out. I wanted Jalini to trust me. "And by that, you mean it could suggest General Hughes was murdered?"

Jalini closed her eyes for a second, took a deep breath, and then looked up at me. "For someone in my position, it is easier to do my job and not ask questions. So, that is what I am doing, and it is what I told Rashi to do."

"I understand. I really do. But what if staying quiet means this man has the ability to continue hurting people?"

Jalini's dark eyes bored into me. "You believe the tales?"

"I don't know." This was true. I had no idea what I believed, but the timeline was convenient. The ghost haunting the forest started just about a year before, which was only a few months before the bombing. Was it crazy to think an assassin could have set up a camp in the area in order to secretly go about his evil deeds?

"Neither do I," she said, pressing her lips together and returning to her work of chopping vegetables.

The kitchen door opened and Hannah returned, her mouth turned down in an exaggerated frown. "Mrs. Hutchins said the library was too hot, so I had to open all the windows on the second floor."

"But the birds—" Jalini started.

Hannah nodded before Jalini could finish. "But before I

was even to the bottom of the stairs, she yelled for me to close them to shut out the incessant singing of the birds."

The two women looked at one another and rolled their eyes, and I was pleased they felt comfortable enough to do this in my presence.

"I will leave you two to your work," I said, folding my hands behind my back and walking towards the door. "Tonight at dinner, I will try to convince Mrs. Hutchins that I'm growing thin from all the soup. Perhaps, then, she will allow you to cook something that requires actual preparation."

"Oh, would you?" Hannah asked, eyes hopeful. "That would be a relief."

I waved as I left. "I'll see what I can do."

11

I left a note in Mrs. Hutchins' room that I would be late for dinner—knowing she wouldn't see it until she got up from her spot in the library and went to her bedroom to change for dinner—and left. My investigation into the possible presence of an assassin in Simla had been insubstantial thus far. I had two vague descriptions and a handful of unrelated evidence, but nothing solid. I was desperate for anything that could let me know I had not allowed paranoia and stress to turn my mind. So, I headed for the western edge of the settlement where the ghost Jalini told me about was supposed to live.

It was possible I was chasing a folktale, an imaginary figure whispered about to invoke fear and fill an evening with good conversation. But the ghost was all I had to go off of, so I had to try.

As soon as I stepped from the main path and into the trees, I was glad I'd gone during daylight. The foliage from the trees was thick and shaded so that it looked like dusk rather than midday. I couldn't imagine how dark it would be at night.

I walked until my feet began to ache, and a larger part of me wanted to turn back and go home than potentially uncover evidence of an assassin. Luckily, it was at this point that I saw a small break in the trees.

It was an almost imperceptible opening in the foliage, like a curtain pulled ever so slightly back by a curious hand, but it was there. I moved towards it and with every step, the outline of a hut became clearer. The roof had been disguised with dried pine branches and the walls were made of dirt and sticks so it would blend into the trees. For anyone not looking for a structure, it would be easy to miss.

I moved behind a tree and waited, listening to the sway of the branches above me, to the flutter of bird's wings, and the soft crackling of the forest floor beneath the wildlife. I closed my eyes and gave myself over to my sense of hearing, waiting for any sign that I was not alone, for any sign that I should turn and run. But there was nothing. Just the gentle sounds of nature. So, I stepped out from behind the tree and moved towards the hut.

My heart hammered in my chest with every step. What if the hut was occupied by an insane man who lived alone and didn't like being disturbed? I suddenly chastised myself for coming without a weapon. I'd been so excited by the possibility of a clue that I'd left the Hutchins' bungalow armed with nothing but the clothes on my back and my curiosity. Neither of which would do me any good in a hand-to-hand fight.

I walked around all four sides of the small hut, which took less than thirty paces all together because the structure was so small, and didn't see any other doors or windows other than the one leading in through the front. There was one way in and one way out. If someone was hiding inside, I was sure to encounter them. They wouldn't be able to slip out the back unseen. Knowing the longer I took to enter, the less brave I would become, I took a deep breath and pressed on the rough-hewn wooden door. It opened inward, and I stepped inside.

The room was dark without any windows, but a small shaft of light cut in from the front door, splitting the room in two. One look around, and it was obvious I was alone. For now. To avoid meeting the owner of the hut, I decided to make my visit there brief. Wasting no time, I began looking around.

Immediately, I noticed the large number of weapons. The entire right side of the hut was devoted to hammers, axes, and a bow and arrow hanging from the mud walls. A small wooden table sat in the middle of the room and was covered in lengths of rope, ammunition, and several small pistols.

Whoever owned the hut, their purpose was not to enjoy a simple getaway from the bustling town. No, the hut was meant to be used as storage. A hiding place for weapons so the person could have relatively easy access to them without needing to keep them on his person or in his place of residence.

I considered taking one of the pistols to use as protection should the owner return, but something stopped me. Perhaps, the idea that the gun could have taken innocent lives or that grabbing it and taking it with me would tie me to the assassin in ways I was not yet ready for. Either way, I turned away from the table and looked towards the left side of the hut.

The final wall was quite unlike the others. Rather than weapons, I was met with long sheaths of fabrics in various colors. It wasn't until I saw an embroidered belt that I recognized the long pieces of cotton as a traditional *dhoti*. So, the owner of the hut was a native. I thought so, at least, until I saw a box sitting in the corner. Inside were brown pastes and powders, as well as several towels covered in dark smears. Makeup.

The *dhoti* and the makeup were there to disguise the assassin as a local Indian man. He came to the hut to disguise his appearance when necessary and grab weapons, which he would probably hide in the deep folds of his outfit.

I stepped away from the wall and spun around the room, taking in everything. The man could be anyone. The descriptions given by Rashi and the man convicted of the Beckingham bombing meant nothing if the assassin had been in disguise. He could be someone I'd passed in the city. Someone I'd spoken to.

Suddenly, I couldn't spend another second inside the hut. I had to get out. I had to step back into the daylight and surround myself with people, regardless of whether I could trust them or not. The sense that I had taken on something much too large to handle was overwhelming, and I felt like I couldn't breathe.

I was stumbling towards the door when I noticed a knife hanging by the door from a hook. Unlike everything else in the room, the knife and the hook were polished to a shine, pristine. The blade was curved at an unusual angle and etched with vines and leaves that moved downwards and carried over to the handle where raised wood mimicked the feeling of vines beneath the user's palm. At the bottom was a mark with two interwoven C's. It was a beautiful weapon, easily the most distinguished in the room. And clearly, based upon how the owner cared for it, it was important.

Before I could think better of it, I grabbed the knife from the hook, stashed it beneath my sweater, and ran through the door and into the trees without looking back.

RELIEF FLOODED through me as soon as I was back in town and surrounded by people. It was almost possible to believe walking through the hut had been a dream, but the cold press of the knife against my skin reminded me it had been all too real.

At lunch, Lieutenant Collins had mentioned he would be near the city hall for the rest of the afternoon, and I found myself walking there without realizing it. I wandered into the building, smiling and nodding as I passed men in suits who eyed me and my walking skirt and sweater with curiosity. I was underdressed.

"Do you know where Lieutenant Graham Collins might be?" I asked a woman sitting behind a large wooden desk in the lobby.

She furrowed her brow and looked down at the desk and then back at me. "Is he an employee? Do you know which department he might be in?"

"I'm not sure—" I started, only to be interrupted by a familiar voice.

"Rose?"

I turned to see none other than Lieutenant Collins standing behind me. I waved to the secretary and walked towards him.

"What are you doing here?" he asked. Then, he shook his head. "That makes it sound like I am not delighted to see you, which I absolutely am. What a surprise. Running into you twice in one day."

"Well, it's hardly a surprise for me since I came here in search of you," I said.

The smile that spread across his face was enough to send a shot of guilt through me. His fondness for me would run out if I continued leading him to believe my feelings for him were as strong as his for me. I had to be careful moving forward to protect his heart and our budding friendship.

"I have a question," I added quickly, glancing around to be sure no one was eavesdropping.

His eyes widened in curiosity, his smile restrained yet eager. "What is it in regard to?"

"Something I found. I think you may have a better idea of its origins than I would, so I came to seek your opinion."

The smile faltered. "All right. Let's sit, shall we?"

"Somewhere private," I said as he began moving towards a table in the lobby.

Lieutenant Collins' face pulled together in suspicion, and then he took a sharp left through the doors of the building and into the square. I followed him around the corner of the building and down a walkway bordered by thick trees on either side. At the end, it opened into a small landscaped garden with stone benches. He gestured for me to take a seat and then sat next to me, our legs close enough to touch.

"I must admit, Miss Beckingham, you have piqued my curiosity."

"Then I won't draw out the suspense another moment," I said, reaching under the top layer of my dress and pulling out the weapon.

Lieutenant Collins paled and looked away as I fumbled with my cardigan and the material of my skirt. His cheeks were bright red by the time I was finished. I feared I had scandalized him. But my potential indiscretion was forgotten the moment he laid eyes on the weapon in my hands.

"Miss Beckingham," he said, sliding away from me as though he was afraid I would use the knife on him. "What was that doing beneath your clothes?"

"I found it." I didn't know how much to tell him about the hut in the woods. He was a sensible, kind man, and my propensity for finding danger would overwhelm him eventually. And it was my wish that his breaking point would be farther in the future. As it was, he had been a valuable resource I had no desire to lose.

He raised an eyebrow and his blonde mustache twitched similar to the way Monsieur Prideaux's used to when I was irritating him. "You found it?"

I nodded. "In the woods. And I wondered if you could tell me more about it."

He looked like he would much rather walk back down the pathway and into the building, forgetting any of this had happened, but when I held the knife out to him, the Lieutenant reluctantly grabbed it and held it in his hands carefully.

"It is called a *kukri*."

"You know it, then?" I asked excitedly, placing a hand on his arm.

He softened under my touch. "I do. They are often carried by Gurkha soldiers, though anyone can acquire one should they wish to."

The disappointment must have been obvious on my face because Lieutenant Collins lowered the knife into his lap. "Does this have something to do with our trip to the prison? Do you believe this knife could somehow be connected to the bomber?"

I opened my mouth and then closed it, unsure how to tell Lieutenant Collins that I believed the wrong man had been convicted for the crime, that I thought the real attacker may still be free and dangerous.

Lieutenant Collins turned towards me and reached for my hand. "I think you have done enough searching for this man, Rose. I do not want to impose because this journey is yours alone, but I worry you may become consumed by this. I'm sorry you were not able to see the man in person, but you are chasing a ghost."

Not wanting to lie to him or admit the full breadth of my investigation, I smiled and refocused the conversation. "What about this engraving on the bottom of the knife? Have you ever seen anything like this? Could it point to who the owner of the knife was?"

He sighed, aware that I did not intend to take his well-intentioned advice, and turned the knife point down to study the butt of the handle. "Oh, the intertwined C's? No, that is just a marking to let the buyer know the knife was inspected in Calcutta. It is a beautiful, well cared for blade, but there is no way to say who it could have belonged to."

"Thank you anyway," I said. "I'm sorry to interrupt your day with this."

"You did not interrupt anything, Miss Beckingham," he said, returning the knife to me. "Though, I would occasionally like to meet with you under normal circumstances."

"Normal how?" I asked, giving him a small smile. "I'm only teasing. I apologize for dragging you into my personal journey for closure. I promise to do my best to find information on my own from now on."

"Or, perhaps," he said, chewing on his lower lip. "You could give up this quest for information all together?"

"I thought you weren't going to impose," I said, the words sharper than I intended.

He shook his head. "You are right. I'm overstepping. It is just that I worry about you, Rose. About the kind of people you will encounter during your search for...whatever it is you are searching for. It isn't safe."

"I am not putting myself in any serious danger, Lieutenant. Please do not worry about me."

"I do worry, though. I know it may seem harmless, but any kind of investigation into a crime of this magnitude can draw unwanted attention. What if the man who killed your family had accomplices? What if word spreads that you are looking into this and they come after you again?"

Lieutenant Collins was flustered in a way I hadn't seen before. I was flattered he was so nervous for my safety.

"The bombing was a random attack," I reminded him. I didn't necessarily believe this story, but it was in the official report that the Lieutenant would trust. "No one will come after me."

"You cannot know that. Especially with the way you often wander by yourself. You could be attacked while out for a walk or targeted in your home. I just think you are taking this search too far," he snapped.

Tensions were rising between us, and I didn't exactly understand why. "I'm attempting to make sense of a tragedy that killed my parents. I think something like that deserves my full attention."

I was lying, of course, but none of that should have mattered. Lieutenant Collins didn't know I was being dishonest, which made his frankness all the more inappropriate. Though we had become friends, we had not known one another long, and it was rude for him to believe he had any kind of say in my doings.

Lieutenant Collins clenched his jaw and smoothed his hands down the front of his uniform. He couldn't look me in the eyes. "You are right. I will hold my tongue on this matter from here on out."

I tucked the *kukri* beneath my cardigan once again and stood up. "Perhaps, that would be best."

12

Miss Dayes had invited me to a small gathering of the daughters of other officials that night, but after searching the *White Tiger Club*, finding the hut, and getting into an argument with Lieutenant Collins all in the same day, I felt exhausted and longed for nothing more than an evening spent in the quiet of my room.

Arthur Hutchins and his mother had been invited to a party in town, as well, but they had declined the invitation. I only knew because I overheard a heated discussion between Arthur and his secretary, Mr. Barlow, while I was sitting at my desk attempting to write a letter to my cousins. I'd been meaning to write to them and ask about their lives in New York and inform them about my adventures in Morocco and India (leaving out everything to do with my personal investigation), but time had gotten away from me. I was finally penning their names at the top of a page when I heard harsh voices in the hallway. Unable to resist, I moved to my door and pressed my ear against the crack.

"You cannot continue to refuse invitations to these

events," Mr. Barlow said.

Arthur huffed. "Thank you for your input, but I can do as I please."

"This is why you hired me, Mr. Hutchins. You said you needed someone to concern themselves with your social calendar to ensure you maintained the proper amount of involvement. Well, I am telling you now that you are slipping in your obligations."

"If you are so concerned, perhaps you should attend the event in our stead. You were gone all afternoon, so it seems you rather enjoy socializing," Arthur snapped. He took a calming breath and continued. "My mother is unwell here in Simla, and I do not want to tax her by taking another car ride through the mountains."

Everyone knew Miss Hutchins was perfectly well. In fact, I'd seen her leave for a walk directly after dinner, looking rosy-cheeked and chipper. She still paused in the doorway to complain about the "dreadful heat" before leaving, but otherwise, her only problem was a propensity for negative thinking.

"Your mother does not need to attend with you," Mr. Barlow argued. "She is on a walk at the moment. She is feeling quite ready for an outing, I would say. And separately, I think you are doing yourself a disservice by staying out of the public eye for so long."

"Thank you for your opinion, Mr. Barlow, but I must insist you drop the matter. I will be staying in tonight. Feel free to concern yourself with your own social events for the remainder of the day."

I heard a door slam and then, after a long pause, footsteps moving down the hallway before becoming too faint to hear.

The house remained quiet after that, allowing me to

finish the letter to my cousins, where I begged them to forgive me for taking so long to write. Then I reflected on what I'd discovered during my investigations that day.

Major McKinley had caught my attention early in the afternoon, especially after I discovered his cigar cutter in the library where General Hughes had died after he'd claimed to have never stepped foot in the room before the day the body was found. However, Rashi, the servant at the *White Tiger Club*, claimed to have seen a different man in the hallway just before the General's body was discovered. Since she knew Major McKinley well from seeing him around the club, if he had been the man in the hallway that morning, she would have recognized him. And it was Jalini's tale of a mysterious man living in the woods near the city that had taken me to the hut where I'd discovered the knife. Nothing much about the man's identity was learned from my search of the hut, except that he utilized disguises and could be almost anyone.

Most surprising of all, however, had been my conversation with Lieutenant Collins. I'd gone to see my friend because I believed he would be able to tell me about the knife I'd found in the hut—which he had. It was his unsolicited advice for me to cease all searching for the man who had thrown the bomb that killed the Beckinghams that was most noteworthy to me.

The Lieutenant and I did not know one another well, so it seemed surprising to me that he would feel comfortable speaking so openly to me about my choices. Furthermore, my defiance seemed to actually anger him, which was an unusual emotion to see on the man I had come to view as mild-mannered. I couldn't help but wonder whether the Lieutenant wasn't worried about what I would discover.

He had been more than willing to assist me at every

stage of my investigation—asking his peers for information and arranging a visit to the prison. I'd quickly accepted him as an exceptionally generous man, but now I wondered whether there had not been ulterior motives. Had he stuck close to me so he would know if I discovered anything that could be dangerous to him? Or, even worse, had he been lying to me in order to discourage me?

Lieutenant Collins had been the one to inform me that the suspected bomber had been captured and killed, and he had been the one to take me to the prison cell where the man was supposedly held. And the only witness I had confirming the presence of the suspected bomber was his cellmate who only spoke Hindi, which the Lieutenant had been kind enough to translate for me. And finally, he had told me the *kukri* was a common knife and the double-Cs marking the bottom were not distinguishable, but simply meant the weapon had been inspected in Calcutta. He had been the one to turn every one of my leads into a dead end, which left me no choice but to wonder whether I had been wrong to trust him all this time.

I was reading in a chair near the window, trying to take my mind off the investigation, if only for a short while, when I heard a piercing scream.

The book fell from my hands, tumbling to the floor, and I stood up and moved to the window. The path running in front of the house was clear, though I could not see it in its entirety as the sun was mostly set, only the barest hint of orange light peeking over the horizon. Squares of light coming from the windows of the bungalow dotted the yard, illuminating small patches of grass, but each patch was empty.

I stood in the window, scanned the land in front of the house, and began to wonder whether stress hadn't caused me to imagine the entire thing, when suddenly, a shape came stumbling into one of the squares of light. I jolted back in surprise and then drew closer to the window, leaning out of it.

"Hello?" I called. "Are you all right?"

"Help me!" The voice was frantic and high-pitched, and it took me only a second to place it as belonging to Mrs. Hutchins. "I've been attacked!"

I ran from my room, down the stairs, and through the front door, shouting for anyone within hearing range to assist me. I had no idea how badly Mrs. Hutchins was injured or if she was injured at all. Perhaps, she had grown tired of complaining about the heat and had increased the stakes, now faking her own attack. However, as soon as I reached the lawn, I knew she was telling the truth.

Small drips of blood dotted the grass leading to where she was lying on her side, a hand held to her throat.

"Mrs. Hutchins, where are you injured?" I asked, kneeling down next to the woman. I had no medical training and no idea of how to help her, but no one else was appearing, so it seemed likely I would be called upon to take care of her.

"A man came from behind me as I was nearing the house," she choked out, squeezing her eyes shut, fat tears rolling down her wrinkled cheeks. "He carried a knife. I didn't have the opportunity to defend myself."

"He had a knife?" I asked, looking her over to find the source of her bleeding. "Where did he cut you?"

Her hands clutched at her throat. "He went for my neck first, but I managed to stumble away from the blade before it sliced through the air. I do not know if he managed to cut me or not. I ran as fast as I could the moment my shock gave way to panic. I have never been so frightened in all my life."

She was hysterical, her voice coming out in hiccups and sobs. It was difficult to understand her. "Mrs. Hutchins, you need to calm down so I can help you."

"You are not a doctor," she snapped. "I need a physician."

"You may be bleeding to death," I shot back. "As we are still alone despite your screaming, I may be the only help coming. Please, tell me where you are hurt."

She clawed at her neck and her scalp in search of the wound before she sat up and I spotted it myself.

"Your back." I reached out and smoothed the material of her dress. A large red splotch covered most of her right shoulder, and it was growing bigger by the minute.

Her eyes went wide. "Have I been stabbed? Am I mortally wounded? I knew I should have stayed inside. What was I thinking, being out alone after dark?"

I probed the wound with my fingers and then pulled Mrs. Hutchins' collar aside to examine it more closely. The blade that had sliced her had been sharp and, had the attacker been able to exert complete control over her, it could have been lethal. But because she had fought back and ran, she saved herself. I told her as much, though it did little to comfort her.

"We need to get inside at once," she said, hauling herself to her feet faster than I'd seen her move in any of the preceding days since we'd been in Simla. "The attacker could still be nearby. I need to find my son. Arthur!"

The idea hadn't even occurred to me. I'd been so concerned with Mrs. Hutchins' safety that I had paid no thought for my own. I glanced around the property, focusing my eyes on the shadows between the trees, but no movement caught my attention.

"Arthur!" she screamed even louder. I couldn't imagine

how her son had not heard her initial screams. Her voice was echoing off the trees. I felt certain it was echoing off the buildings in town.

"Screaming may draw the attacker back," I said, looping my arm through Mrs. Hutchins' and assisting her towards the house. "He may believe he delivered a mortal wound and return when he hears you screaming and learns otherwise.

She shook her head. "No, he knew I survived."

"How can you be sure?" I asked.

"After he first tried to attack me, I fended him off and then turned around. The moment he saw my face, he ran in the opposite direction."

My brows knit together, attempting to sort out this puzzle. "You mean, the man ran away from *you*?"

She called for her son again, ignoring my request for her to cease screaming, and then panted out an affirmation. "I could not see his face as it was hidden in shadow from the large hood he was wearing, but I heard the sound of surprise when he saw my face. He must not have expected an old woman to be so quick. I can hardly believe I was able to run and carry on the way I did."

"A hood?"

Mrs. Hutchins circled her hands around her face several times. "A complex wrap of some kind. It draped across his shoulders and hung down his body in rags. It could scarcely be considered clothes."

I hummed a response, too deep in thought to respond properly.

Mrs. Hutchins did look quite young. Despite her frequent complaining about her age and the heat and the toll things as simple as going up and down the stairs could have on her body, she was quite thin and fit. We had similar builds, in fact. And draped in a lacy blue dress, it was easy to see how someone could have mistaken her for someone younger...someone like me.

The thought sent a chill down my spine, and I looked over my shoulder, ensuring no one was sneaking up the walk behind us. Mrs. Hutchins was still screaming, but suddenly I didn't want to stop her. I wanted someone else to come along and find us. A larger group would better ensure our safety.

The man who had attacked her had been wearing rags that concealed his identity. And as soon as he'd seen her face, he'd run away. How many conclusions could I possibly draw? I did not want to force the facts to fit my narrative, but very little force was necessary. It seemed most plausible that the man who had attacked Mrs. Hutchins was the same man whose hut I had been in only hours before. And perhaps, was the same man who had thrown the bomb in the city square that ended the lives of Mr. and Mrs. Beckingham, their daughter, and their driver.

Had the attack occurred the night before, I would have been dubious of leaping to such a conclusion, but since I had been in the assassin's secret hut that afternoon and left with what was clearly a cherished weapon, it was not surprising that he had come to hunt me down. Perhaps, he felt my investigation was becoming uncomfortable for him. Maybe he believed I was close to solving the mystery of his identity. Or maybe he believed I was beginning to interfere with his next target.

Possibilities swirled in my head as Mrs. Hutchins and I approached the bungalow and Arthur finally came out of the house, rubbing his hand down his face like he'd just woken up.

"There you are," Mrs. Hutchins cried, stumbling up the

stairs despite my arm to lend her additional balance. She threw herself at her son who responded by holding his arms straight out, refusing to engage in the embrace.

"Did I hear someone scream?" he asked.

"Several times." Annoyance was obvious in my voice. Mr. Barlow's lecture to him in the hallway about leaving the house had clearly not made any kind of impression. His own mother had nearly been murdered behind the bungalow, and he'd waited nearly five minutes to stand up and respond to the screaming.

"I was attacked," Mrs. Hutchins began, grabbing her son's arms and looking out towards the front garden as if she expected her attacker to be pursuing her. "Rose tells me I am wounded, though I am too much in shock to feel any pain."

Arthur leaned around his mother, inspecting her for injuries while she relayed the story to him.

"We ought to call for a doctor," he said coldly. "Rose, would you be so kind as to fetch a servant who could—"

He stopped mid-sentence and brushed me aside with a wave of his mind. "Never mind. I'll ask Mr. Barlow to help."

I followed his gaze and saw Mr. Barlow walking along the same path Mrs. Hutchins had been on, though from the opposite direction. His head was down, staring at his feet as he kicked up dirt along the path.

"Hurry along, Mr. Barlow," Arthur called to his secretary. "We've had a bit of excitement while you were away."

"A bit of excitement?" Mrs. Hutchins repeated, clearly disgusted.

Mr. Barlow looked up, noticed us on the porch, and increased his walking pace. While we waited for him to join us, Mrs. Hutchins and her son argued back and forth about the seriousness of the matter and how he had no respect for her life or safety.

"What has happened? I was only on a short walk," he said, as though trying to explain to his employer why he hadn't been immediately available to assist with the matter.

Mrs. Hutchins seemed glad to retell her story for the third time. Arthur jumped in several times to speed her along. She'd begun to embellish certain story elements. Mr. Barlow heard a version where the attacker looped his arm around Mrs. Hutchins' neck and tried to choke her before she was able to weasel away and escape.

"Thank heavens you are safe," he said. It was a strange dichotomy to hear him speak genuine words with such a flat tone. "I will send for a doctor immediately."

Mrs. Hutchins threw a hand to her forehead like a Victorian lady. "I think I need to lie down."

"If you lie down, you will ruin the furniture," her son said, showing little familial concern for his mother's knife wound. "The bungalow is only leased to us, I'll remind you. Wherever you sit, keep your back from touching the fabrics."

"Your mother has nearly been slain, and you are concerned about the cost of replacing furniture. Arthur Hutchins, you should be ashamed of yourself. That your secretary and a woman I met only days ago would show more compassion towards me in my time of need is shocking."

Arthur was unaffected by his mother's assessment of the situation, and by the time we got inside and the servants were gathering to see what the commotion was about, Mrs. Hutchins was too busy relaying her tale yet again to worry at all about her son.

Mr. Barlow spoke in a low tone to Jalini, who offered me

a pointed look when she heard Mrs. Hutchins describe the attacker's appearance and attire. I knew she had come to the same conclusion as I had, but there was no time for us to discuss the matter. As there was no telephone in the house, Jalini left immediately, tasked with fetching a doctor back to the bungalow for Mrs. Hutchins.

Jalini had only been gone a few minutes when there was a loud pounding on the front door. The sitting room, which moments before had been bustling with servants bringing the lady of the house warm towels and water and Mrs. Hutchins shouting at Arthur to come back downstairs and care for his mother, went silent.

"Could that be the doctor already?" I asked.

Three more knocks rattled the solid wooden door on its hinges, yet no one moved to answer the door. No one had said so explicitly, but I could sense the collective nervousness of everyone in the home. There were too many unanswered questions for anyone to relax. Why had Mrs. Hutchins been attacked and by whom? Would the attacker return to finish the job or had it been random? Was anyone else in the home also in danger?

Not wanting to listen to another round of knocking on the front door, I passed the frozen servants in the sitting room and stepped into the entrance hall alone. On the slight chance the attacker had come back, I knew he would be there for me, and I didn't want anyone else to get hurt in my stead. So, gathering my courage, I took a deep breath and pulled the door open.

Standing in front of the door, fist raised in the air, prepared to knock again, was none other than Lieutenant Collins. When he saw I was the one who had answered the door, his face paled.

13

I took two stumbling steps away from the door, unsure if the Lieutenant was going to lunge towards me or not.

Why had he come here so late in the evening and without any notice? In my mind, there was only one possibility: Lieutenant Collins was the assassin.

It all made sense now. He had taken an immediate liking to me when he'd come to the Hutchins' bungalow for lunch the first full day I was in Simla. It had always seemed strange to me that a young, single man like Lieutenant Collins would spend his time with the likes of the Hutchins', but if he had been there in order to get closer to me, then it made perfect sense. Also, he had been much too willing to assist me with the investigation. In my naiveté, I'd assumed he was an exceptionally kind man, but when would I learn men were never kinder than they needed to be?

But our conversation that very afternoon stood out clearest in my mind. I had gone to him because I trusted him, because I believed he would answer my questions without prying too far. However, the Lieutenant had pried into my business and become quite angry in the process. At the time, I'd thought perhaps it was because of his concern for me and my safety, but now I understood the truth. Lieutenant Collins recognized the knife because it belonged to him. The double-Cs marking the bottom of the handle probably represented his surname—Collins. Lieutenant Collins saw the knife, knew I had been in his hut in the woods, and knew it would only be a matter of time before he could no longer lead me astray with lies that pointed to dead ends and a smile. So, he had come to the Hutchins' bungalow to put an end to me.

However, instead of slashing my neck, he had attacked Mrs. Hutchins. For reasons that still weren't clear, he had decided to spare her, as she was not his intended target, and now he was back at the house in search of me.

As this new reality washed over me, Lieutenant Collins stepped forward and placed his hands on my shoulders. I was frozen in shock and fear.

"There is blood on the steps, Rose," he said, eyes wide. "Whose is it? Are you injured?"

"Oh, Lieutenant," Mrs. Hutchins called from the other room. "Thank heavens you are here. We need a strong man around right now."

This seemed to be a pointed insult at Arthur, but I could hardly pay attention to what anyone was saying. The killer was in the house. He was standing right in front of me. Touching me. What was I meant to do about it?

"Who is injured?" he asked, looking around the room wildly for an answer, as though he didn't already know.

"Mrs. Hutchins received a slash to her back," Mr. Barlow said, stepping forward. "We've already sent for a doctor."

Lieutenant Collins nodded and looked back at me, breathing heavily. His shoulders pitched forward in relief, and he lowered his head to speak to me. Suddenly, with him standing over me, I could picture his face beneath a large hood. I could see him running through the streets of Simla with a bomb hidden beneath his coat. The face that had eluded me for so many months seemed to be growing clearer in my mind. Had there been a blonde mustache on the assassin's face? Perhaps. I thought I could remember it now.

"I came to see you, Rose. I wanted to apologize."

"Apologize for what, Lieutenant?" I asked, voice shaking as I stepped away from him, out of his reach. Apologize for killing my family? For murdering innocent people?

Confusion crossed his face when I moved away from him, but he made no move to follow. Lieutenant Collins dropped his arms to his side and stood tall, his shoulders pushed back. "For the way I spoke to you this afternoon. I understand it was uncouth. I do not know whether it is in my defense to note that I realized my behavior was rude in the moment or not. It has not taken me this many hours to understand why I was wrong. But it has taken me this long to come to the realization that you are a grown woman who will make her own decision regardless of my concerns. I should not have attempted to control you."

"Thank you, Lieutenant." I wanted to speak normally to him. I did not want him to realize anything was amiss because I did not yet know what I was going to do with the information that he was likely the assassin I'd been searching for. I did not have any hard proof, so there was little I could do. However, my voice sounded strained even to my own ears. Being near him felt impossible. I couldn't resist wrapping my arms around myself and pulling away from him.

The Lieutenant tucked his lower lip into his mouth, his

mustache twitching to one side. "I know I have upset you, Rose. I do not seek your immediate forgiveness now, but I do hope you will be able to forgive me eventually so we can carry on as we once did. I do not want my own loud mouth to hinder our friendship."

I curled my fingers into a fist, fighting the urge to slap him for his lies, for his deception. I had to find proof. I had to find something that could conclusively link Lieutenant Collins to the bombing or the murder of General Hughes. Anything that could keep him off the streets and away from his hut of weapons and disguises in the forest.

"Of course, nothing will hinder our friendship," I said softly. Each word physically hurt to speak. "I can forgive your frank discussion of your opinions if you can forgive my eccentricities."

In the span of a few seconds, Lieutenant Collins was directly in front of me again, cupping my hands in his. It was too late to pull away, so I focused my eyes on the wall over his shoulder and waited for it to be over. "It is not eccentric to want to make peace with the passing of your family. Your life has been so irrevocably altered in this last year, and it was wrong of me to think it was my place to tell you how that peace should be found. Continue searching with the knowledge that I will be here to support you."

I was saved the task of responding when the oft-quiet Mr. Barlow moved to the center of the sitting room and waved his arms, directing people away from Mrs. Hutchins. "The room should be cleared for the doctor's arrival. He will need space to work."

Lieutenant Collins let go of my hands and moved to stand behind Mrs. Hutchins. "Are you in pain, Mrs. Hutchins? Is there anything that can be done for you until the doctor arrives?"

The woman sighed and looked up at the Lieutenant with a smile. For a second, I imagined a look of horror would cross her face, flashes of memory from her ordeal coming back to her. I imagined her recognizing the Lieutenant and screaming, begging for him to be removed from the home and locked away. None of that happened, of course. She reached back and patted her hand over his where it lay on the back of the sofa. "I do not know how you found yourself here so quickly after my trauma, Lieutenant, but I am glad for it. The comfort I feel at your presence is much greater."

If only she knew the truth, I thought.

Mr. Barlow was still standing in the middle of the room, frowning now. He glanced towards me, his eyes black and unseeing before he turned back to Mrs. Hutchins. "Madam, perhaps everyone except those currently residing in the house should leave. I mean no disrespect, Lieutenant, but Mrs. Hutchins was violently attacked and the culprit has not been apprehended. It might be wise to keep the outside world away from the home until we learn more about what happened."

Mrs. Hutchins gasped, tightening her grip on Lieutenant Collins' hand. "Mr. Barlow, are you suggesting Lieutenant Collins may have been the monster who slashed me?"

Mr. Barlow sighed, closing his eyes for a moment to gather his thoughts. "I'm not accusing him. Only noting that it may be wise to keep guests away from—"

"I refuse to live in fear of my own friends," Mrs. Hutchins said, sticking out her jaw in defiance. "That is what my attacker wanted. His goal was to scare me into exile, and I refuse to allow it."

I stepped forward now, eyes locked on the Lieutenant.

"Actually, Mrs. Hutchins, I believe your attacker's goal was to end your life."

He had no reaction to my words, but Mrs. Hutchins blanched at the idea before shaking her head. "Regardless, the Lieutenant is more than welcome to stay."

"I am glad my presence can bring you some level of comfort," Lieutenant Collins said. Then, he turned to face me and Mr. Barlow. "However, if leaving would make things easier, then I am happy to go home and return tomorrow to check on you."

"Absolutely not," Mrs. Hutchins cried. "In fact, I was considering asking you to stay in our guest room, Lieutenant. It can't hurt to have a military man staying in the house to protect us. After all, I am an old, and now injured, woman, Rose is but a delicate young lady, and Arthur is nowhere to be found. I fear we are ripe for the picking should the attacker return."

Lieutenant Collins studied me for a second, gauging my reaction to Mrs. Hutchins' suggestion. I was too numb to have much of a response, and Lieutenant Collins shrugged. "I will do whatever would be most helpful to everyone in the home. If staying the night would increase your comfort, then I'm happy to do it."

Mr. Barlow's brow lowered, and he opened his mouth to argue, but then the door burst open. The doctor had arrived.

Mrs. Hutchins' wound was described as superficial by the doctor—a diagnosis Mrs. Hutchins found insulting.

"A superficial wound would not cause this amount of blood loss," she insisted, pointing to the stain on the sofa, which Arthur set several servants to cleaning at once. "My hand tingles and I cannot lift my arm over my head. My mobility may be altered forever. Does that sound superficial?"

Lieutenant Collins took up a post in a chair near the window, watching over the front garden diligently. Had I not believed him to be the very culprit he was searching for, I may have fallen for his act as our protector. To avoid being too near him, I busied myself getting whatever Mrs. Hutchins required, which ranged from more blankets to keep her feet warm to bundles of ice to cool her forehead. She couldn't seem to decide whether being too warm or too cold was more sympathetic, so she settled on being both.

Everyone knew she was being overly dramatic, but no one could say so without being insensitive. Besides, I knew the attacker had mistaken her for me, so I felt it was my duty to make her as comfortable as possible in repayment. For all of her faults, Mrs. Hutchins had invited me to travel with her to Simla and allowed me to stay in her home at no cost. It was an incredibly kind offer that had brought trouble to her doorstep. Or, in the case of Lieutenant Collins, to her sitting room.

As the evening wore on, even Mrs. Hutchins grew tired of all the attention and stood up from the sofa with a great deal more effort than was necessary.

"Rose, could you help me to my room?" she asked, holding out a hand. "I need to rest."

I wrapped an arm around her waist and began escorting her towards the stairs when I felt a presence behind me. I looked over my shoulder to see Lieutenant Collins following us.

"I do not believe your assistance will be required, Lieutenant. I can help Mrs. Hutchins just fine on my own," I said.

"No, no. Do come, Lieutenant," Mrs. Hutchins said. "I'd like for you to check the upstairs for me."

"Check for what exactly?" I asked.

"I was just attacked, Rose," she bit back. "I am more than a little uneasy sleeping alone in my room. It would comfort me greatly to have the room looked over first."

"I'm happy to help in any way I can," Lieutenant Collins said, sounding as unflappably helpful as ever.

What was his aim? He had stuck close to me all evening, not allowing me out of his direct line of sight. Was he planning to attack me inside the bungalow with servants watching? Did he think I was going to jump from a second story window and disappear into the night?

Then, I was struck with a realization. Lieutenant Collins knew I had found him out. He knew I suspected him of playing some role in the attack, and he was afraid I would tell someone if I was left alone long enough. I shivered, the hairs standing up on the back of my neck, but I did my best to act natural just as I had all evening. I had to formulate a plan.

"The doctor told you not to sleep on your back," Mr. Barlow called from the bottom of the stairs. "And to prop yourself up to a seated position."

"Rose remembers all of that," Mrs. Hutchins said, waving away Mr. Barlow. "Don't you Rose?"

In fact, I didn't. I hadn't listened to a word the doctor had said while he was in the house examining Mrs. Hutchins. I'd been far too focused on studying Lieutenant Collins.

"I need to speak with Mr. Hutchins, anyway. I'll come help you get settled," Mr. Barlow said, moving silently up the stairs behind us.

"Honestly, you all are making such a fuss over me. I'm so

embarrassed," Mrs. Hutchins said, a pleased smile spreading across her face.

As I kept Mrs. Hutchins steady and upright—a task she certainly could have accomplished on her own—Lieutenant Collins thoroughly checked behind every curtain, inside the closet, and underneath her bed. He shook the windows in their frames to be sure they were locked tight and pulled the drapes closed. Mr. Barlow laid a towel down on the bed and once again reminded Mrs. Hutchins not to lie on her back, to keep three pillows under her at all times, and to have a servant change her wrapping first thing in the morning to avoid infection. Then, we stepped into the hallway and left Mrs. Hutchins to herself.

The three of us made an unusual, uncomfortable group. I wanted only to be alone to try and gather my thoughts and formulate a plan about how to deal with Lieutenant Collins, but Lieutenant Collins refused to leave me alone. And Mr. Barlow, who had said he needed to speak with his employer hadn't made a single move towards Arthur's study door, but instead was straightening the rug that ran the length of the hallway. When he finished that, he stood up and looked at me briefly before crossing his arms and blinking his round, sunken eyes twice.

"Do you think she will be all right for the evening by herself?" Mr. Barlow asked me. "I am worried she may roll over in her sleep and hurt the wound."

"It is only a shallow cut," I said, surprised by his concern. "I'm sure she will be fine."

He nodded, unconvinced, and then raised his eyebrows high, stretching his face into a long, thin mask. "Perhaps, you should stay in her room for the night, Miss Beckingham. That way someone would be there should she wake in the night and need anything."

When had Mr. Barlow come to care so much for Mrs. Hutchins' comfort? In the short time I'd known him, I hadn't seen him express anything other than utter indifference towards Arthur and his mother. Now, suddenly, he worried about Mrs. Hutchins rolling in her sleep in the night.

He was still looking at me, eyes wide and probing, waiting for my response. Was it possible his concern came from a deeper place than just an employee caring for the mother of his employer? Could Mr. Barlow, perhaps...*like* Mrs. Hutchins? The thought was almost laughable, and in fact, I had to suppress a smile.

"I am only down the hall. Should she call in the night, I'll hear her," I said.

"Besides," Lieutenant Collins said more sternly than was necessary, "that kind of thing is why the family employs servants. Rose should not have to sit up all night to care for Mrs. Hutchins. She should sleep in her own bed."

Mr. Barlow grimaced at the Lieutenant for only a second before resuming his apathetic mask. "Of course. Forgive me, Miss. It has been a long night."

"You have nothing to apologize for," I said, giving him a small smile.

"Were you not going to speak with Mr. Hutchins about some matter?" Lieutenant Collins asked.

Mr. Barlow bowed with a sigh and turned to knock on Arthur's study door. After being welcomed inside, he stepped through the door and met my eyes once more before closing it behind him.

Lieutenant Collins took a step closer to me, and I was painfully aware of how small the hallway was. He couldn't very well attack me in the space between two doors, behind which were Mrs. Hutchins and then Arthur and Mr. Barlow. But still, his closeness was threatening.

"I think I also need to rest," I said, moving down the hall towards my room without turning around.

"I shall treat you the way I treated Mrs. Hutchins," he said, following me down the hallway.

For one terrifying second, I thought he was referring to the knife wound in her back, and I spun around, heart racing.

"I shall check your room before you go to sleep," he continued. Then, he saw my face and stepped closer, eyes narrowed. "Is everything all right, Rose?"

"Yes. Absolutely fine."

"It is all right to be frightened," he said, laying a hand on my shoulder. "You've been through a lot tonight."

I moved backwards towards my door, stepping out of his reach once again. "I'm not frightened. Only tired."

Lieutenant Collins nodded in understanding. "Of course. Allow me to check your room and then you should get some rest. It has been a very exciting day for you."

He seemed to be making reference to more than just the evening's activities, probably thinking of our lunch at the *White Tiger Club* along with our meeting in the afternoon when I'd showed him the *kukri*. I wanted to tell him it had been an eventful day for him, too. Between following me to the *White Tiger Club*, attacking Mrs. Hutchins, and spending his evening in the Hutchins' bungalow plotting how to get me alone, he had been quite busy. But I held my tongue.

"That really isn't necessary," I said, opening my door and stepping inside, attempting to push it closed.

Lieutenant Collins slid his boot between the door and the frame, keeping me from closing it. "Please, Rose. It will take only a moment. I truly must insist."

With that, he pushed my door open and stepped inside. I backed away from him, wishing I hadn't come upstairs at all. Perhaps, I should have taken up the offer made by Mr. Barlow to sleep in Mrs. Hutchins' room. Thinking I was safe alone in my own room for the night with the Lieutenant sleeping under the same roof had been foolish.

Lieutenant Collins smiled at me as he pushed the door closed behind him. We were finally alone.

14

I looked around the room for a weapon of any kind. Something sharp, heavy, easy to swing. But there was nothing. I'd travelled to Simla with very few personal items, and the room had been mostly empty when I'd arrived. The *kukri* I'd stolen from the hut was beyond my reach, shut in a locked trunk at the foot of the bed. The key to the lock was inside the desk drawer. I wouldn't have time to get the key and unlock the trunk before Lieutenant Collins was upon me.

"Forgive my insistence, Rose," Lieutenant Collins said, beginning to walk along the edge of my room. "After seeing the blood on the front porch and thinking it belonged to you, I want to do whatever I can to ensure you are safe."

My heart thundered against my ribs, and I hoped the Lieutenant couldn't hear it. "Mrs. Hutchins was the victim, so there is really nothing to worry about."

Lieutenant Collins pulled open my closet and checked inside. Finding it empty, he turned back to me and shook his head. "Rose, I know you do not believe that."

"You think you know my mind better than I do?" I asked.

He smiled, tilting his head to the side. I hated how kind he still looked. "Of course not. I only mean that you are a smart woman, and I'm sure you've come to the same conclusion I have."

This was it. He was going to confess, and I had no idea how I would respond. "And what conclusion would that be?"

He rattled my window the same way he had Mrs. Hutchins'. "That Mrs. Hutchins was mistaken for you. Someone came here in search of you and found her instead."

"That seems like quite the stretch," I said. Perhaps, if I pretended his theory was beyond the realm of possibility, he would believe I didn't truly suspect him.

He turned to me, face stern. "I know you've been lying to me about the reason you came back to Simla."

I could feel sweat gathering along my back. Everything inside of me told me to run, but my feet wouldn't move.

"You say you are looking for closure, but your search is much too focused for something so general," he said. "I do not know exactly what you are searching for, but I know you have been asking around about General Hughes' suicide and I know you went to speak with Elizabeth Hughes."

"Have you been following me?" I asked. How could I have missed him? I prided myself on being observant, on noticing small details. How could I have allowed myself to be followed?

He shook his head. "No, but I know a lot of people in this city, and I've been worried about you, Rose."

"You do not need to worry about me," I snapped.

"Yes, I do," he said. "You do not know what you are getting yourself involved in. I know you endured a tragedy few can imagine when your family was killed, but involving yourself in other deaths and trying to find a murderer where there isn't one will not bring your family back to you. I worry that by asking questions about the wrong people, you will get yourself in trouble."

Once again, Lieutenant Collins didn't want me to investigate any further. Not into the death of General Hughes or into the bombing that killed the Beckinghams. How had I not understood his motives sooner?

"Do you know who those 'wrong people' might be, Lieutenant?"

Lieutenant Collins stepped forward, and I just knew he would confess. This would be the moment when I would have to decide if I was going to scream and beg for help from Mr. Barlow or Arthur Hutchins, or if I was going to fight off Lieutenant Collins by myself.

"If I knew who they were, I wouldn't be so worried about you. I know it may seem too soon for such a declaration, but I care for you very deeply, Rose."

I stood frozen in the middle of the room, unsure of what to say.

The Lieutenant sighed. "Please do not feel the need to respond now. You have been through a difficult day, and I swore to myself I would not bombard you with my feelings. I just need you to know that my concern for you is not because I believe you are incapable of handling yourself. On the contrary, I believe you are an incredibly strong, capable woman. Rather, after the traumas you have already endured, I want a simple life for you," he said, taking small steps towards me. "Perhaps, a life with me."

Lieutenant Collins was getting closer to me, and I had the overwhelming sense that he was going to kiss me. It was the last thing I wanted, but I felt incapable of escaping the situation. If I refused him, I didn't know how he would respond. Would he drop his charade and confess his crimes? Or was he still trying to play the role of my loyal new friend? Too many thoughts and possibilities swirled in my mind, making it impossible to make a decision.

He was only a few steps from me now, and I stared at him, eyes wide, heart racing. I needed a second to collect myself, to wade through the tumultuous sea of emotions raging inside of me. But there was no time. No escape.

"Oh, Rose!" I heard my name through the wall and it took me a few seconds to realize it was coming from the room next door. From Mrs. Hutchins' room. "Are you still awake, dear?"

Lieutenant Collins looked towards the wall and sighed, squeezing his eyes shut for a second, disappointed. I, however, was elated.

"Mrs. Hutchins needs me. Thank you for checking the room, Lieutenant. I will see you in the morning." I dashed from the room, down the hall, and into the room of Mrs. Hutchins.

The woman simply needed me to pull her covers up over her.

"Leaning forward to grab the blankets puts an awful strain on my wound, and I'm afraid I may pull it open again. And lying on my side like this does not help. My hips are already aching," she complained.

I nodded in fake sympathy, wishing she would be quiet so I could hear what was happening in the hallway better. I needed to make sure Lieutenant Collins had left my room. If he did not leave, I would spend the night in Mrs. Hutchins' room whether she wanted me to or not. I refused to step back into an enclosed space with him. I couldn't handle it.

Mrs. Hutchins helped me procrastinate by asking me to straighten the blankets she thought were bunched around her feet, to switch out one of her three pillows for another she felt was fluffier, and tip her glass into her mouth so she could have a sip of water. It was as she was drinking from the glass, finally quiet after several minutes of vapid conversation, that I heard my bedroom door close softly and footsteps move down the hallway and down the stairs. Lieutenant Collins was gone.

"Is that all you need, Mrs. Hutchins?"

The woman looked around the room, probably in search of another mundane task I could assist her with, but evidently could think of nothing left. She sighed, disappointed. "I think so, dear. Thank you so much for caring for me so diligently. I think of you as a daughter, you know?"

"That is very sweet," I said, beginning to understand why Arthur Hutchins walked around with a perpetual frown on his face. "I hope you sleep well. I'll be just on the other side of the wall should you need anything."

I poked my head into the hallway to be sure the Lieutenant wasn't waiting for me out there, and then closed Mrs. Hutchins' door and walked towards my own. It was open just a crack, and I looked through it before entering. The room was truly empty. Quickly, I dashed into my room and locked the door behind me. Just as Lieutenant Collins had done before confessing his "feelings" for me, I walked the perimeter of the room, checking my closet, behind every curtain, and under the bed. After several minutes, I finally felt confident I was alone and dropped onto the edge of my bed, exhausted.

Lieutenant Collins had been right when he'd said I'd had a busy day. I'd planned for the evening to be a relaxing one where I would read and then turn in early, but that was far from how things had turned out. Instead, I'd spent most of the evening making Mrs. Hutchins comfortable and had learned the one person in all of Simla I'd considered a friend had actually been an enemy. I needed a solid night's sleep before I could even begin to figure out what to do next.

Too exhausted to change out of my clothes, I closed my eyes and lay back on the bed. However, as I lay back, I heard something crinkle beneath me. I sat up at once and turned to see a piece of paper lying in the center of the bed. It appeared to be blank.

I couldn't remember whether it had been on the bed earlier in the evening or not. I certainly didn't remember putting it there. As I picked it up, light from the lamp next to my bed passed through it, and I could see that there were words scribbled on the other side. The handwriting was not mine.

My heart lodged itself in my throat, and I took a deep breath before turning the piece of paper over, preparing myself for whatever I would find. Before I could even read the words, I knew that my eventful day had just become even more so. Any possibility of sleep would be gone as soon as I read the message. But that didn't matter. I had to read it. I had to know.

I turned the paper over and gasped.

You already know too much.

15

I shut the note away in the desk drawer as though putting it out of my sight would make it not real.

It was a threat. That much was obvious. But why? Lieutenant Collins could have spoken the words to me when we'd been alone in my room together. Why had he waited to leave the threat until I was next door assisting Mrs. Hutchins? Was it just an attempt to scare me and keep me from investigating further? Or was it a promise of more violence to come? A warning?

I paced around my room until well past midnight. Until the noise of servants and the other occupants in the house faded to silence. Until the only noise I could hear was my own footsteps on the floor.

Where was Lieutenant Collins in the house? There had been little discussion of where he would stay. I knew of a guest room at the back of the house, which seemed the most likely place. But even if that was his room, would he have remained there? Or, was he creeping up the stairs at that very moment, headed for my room? I'd locked my bedroom door, but if he wanted inside, he could find a way.

I couldn't remain in the house another minute.

But I also couldn't leave.

Where would I go? I didn't know anyone else in the city. Miss Dayes was an acquaintance who had seemed fond enough of me to allow me to stay with her for a brief time, but I had no idea where she lived. I knew where Elizabeth Hughes lived, but she hadn't wanted to speak to me under normal circumstances, so I knew she wouldn't want my company once I was on the run from the assassin who had probably killed her father as well as the Beckinghams.

I couldn't run. As much as I wanted to, I had to face this head on. I had to face *him* head on. For eight months, the man who had lobbed the bomb in the Simla marketplace had haunted my nightmares and my waking thoughts. He had been a ghoul, always lurking, waiting for me to lower my guard. But I wouldn't turn and run this time. I would make a plan, and I would be ready to fight.

I grabbed the key from my desk drawer and unlocked the trunk hidden in the closet. The *kukri* was wrapped inside of a blanket. It felt wrong to hold a weapon that had likely been used to kill so many, but if I could turn the blade on its owner, ending his life with the very weapon he had used to kill others, then I could think of no finer justice.

Once the weapon was strapped to my side and hidden beneath a hip-length jacket with a matching tie around the waist, I stood at the door and listened. After several minutes of perfect silence, I found the courage to unlock my door and open it.

The hallway was dark and quiet. The house had been asleep for hours. As far as I could tell, I was the only one awake. Though, I doubted that. The killer was watching, waiting for an opportunity to find me alone. There were too many people still in the house. Too many opportunities for things to go wrong and for their identity to be revealed.

I walked carefully down the hallway, avoiding the center where the boards were the loudest, instead sticking close to the walls. I heard Mrs. Hutchins snoring as I passed her room, and I wondered if I'd see her again. The woman wasn't particularly dear to me, but when faced with the reality that you might be dead within the hour, you become quite nostalgic.

I was at the top of the stairs when I realized I should have left a note for Lord and Lady Ashton, Catherine, and Alice. If I died, I wanted them to know the truth. They deserved that from me.

I had the thought to turn around and scribble out a hasty letter to be sent after my demise, but I resisted the urge. It was more a distraction than anything else. As much as I wanted to confirm Lieutenant Collins as the killer, I wasn't ready to face him. I'd been in several situations where I felt certain I'd die, but still, I'd never been this frightened. Perhaps because in the past, the life or death situations had come as a surprise rather than a plan. I had never walked purposefully into a moment where I knew I'd have to fight for my life; whereas, now my eyes were wide open. I knew what I was doing and all of the potential consequences. I knew there was a possibility I wouldn't see the sunrise. But as scared as I felt, I had to do it. There was no alternative.

Lieutenant Collins had been thorough. There was no proof to convict him of either the murder of General Hughes or the Beckinghams. I could not turn him in to the police because they would have nothing with which to charge him. In fact, all turning him in would accomplish was to discredit myself. People would see me as the scarred survivor of a bombing. As a paranoid woman who needed careful handling and couldn't be trusted. It would ruin my reputation and discredit any future investigative work I could hope to pursue.

I had to face him myself and get a confession. I only hoped I could survive the ordeal.

The stairs squealed beneath my feet, and I winced with each step, certain Lieutenant Collins would be waiting for me at the bottom with a devious smile spread across his face. However, when I turned the corner to move down the final flight of stairs, the landing was empty.

But of course, it was. Lieutenant Collins would not confront me in the house for reasons I had already deduced. He would allow me to escape the house and meet me when I was alone, in a secluded location. I could have slid down the banister and landed in a somersault, and he still would have remained hidden.

The sitting room was dark and vacant, but when I looked down the long hall that ran most of the length of the house, I could see light spilling out from behind one of the doors. It was the hall where most of the servants slept, but it also contained the guest room. I was too far away to see which room the light came from, but I didn't need to see. It would be the guest room. It would be Lieutenant Collins. Lurking behind his closed door, listening to my slow movement through the house, ready to act as soon as his moment arrived.

I felt for the *kukri* hidden beneath my jacket once again for comfort more than anything. To remind myself that I was armed. That I had fought off enemies before, and I could do it again.

As I moved towards the front door, finally ready to leave the relative safety of the bungalow and step out into the moonlight, I noticed the Lieutenant's uniform jacket hanging from the coat rack. A sudden hope flared inside of me, and I rushed for it, digging my hands into the pockets quickly as if I feared someone would appear and scold me for snooping.

Could there be something hidden in the pockets that would connect him to any of his crimes? No. The brief hope fizzled like a candle at the end of its wick. The pockets were empty.

I pulled my hand out, and as I did, I felt something solid through the starched material of the jacket. I opened the flap and ran my hand along the inside of the coat, which was finished in a red satin. There, my fingers felt an opening, a clean break in the material. When I slipped my hand inside, I felt the familiar heft of a pistol. I pulled it out, angling it towards the dim moonlight coming through the entrance hall windows.

Lieutenant Collins had a gun hidden in the inside pocket of his jacket, yet he'd left his jacket in the entrance hall. Why?

From somewhere deep in the house, I heard a floorboard creak, and I knew I didn't have time to stand around and uncover the motives of a madman. I shoved the gun into the pocket of my jacket and backed slowly through the front door, my eyes trained on the long hallway until the door was firmly shut in its frame.

I DIDN'T plan to go to the temple ruins. My feet simply carried me there. It was only a short distance from the bungalow and I was drawn to it as though possessed.

It felt right, though. It was the place I'd first asked Lieutenant Collins for his help, the place I had first confided in him about the trauma of the bombing and my wish for closure. It seemed poignant that the temple would be the same place I found that closure.

Because I was on foot, I approached the temple from the side through a thick crop of trees rather than via the road, which allowed me to hide behind the thicker patches of foliage and watch the courtyard, eyes narrowed for the slightest movement or shift in the air. After waiting long enough that my legs began to cramp and my eyes had grown heavy, I realized the killer would not show himself until I had done so. He operated from the shadows, and in the shadows he would remain until he was certain of my plan.

So, I stood tall, clutched my weapons to my body, and stepped into the courtyard.

It was still dark, the shadows thick at the base of the ruined colonnades, but the moonlight offered enough light to see, and I walked towards the carved stone deity of Hanuman sitting on a pedestal at the center.

There I waited. Minutes ticked by with no movement, no sound, and I began to wonder if I hadn't imagined everything. If my fear hadn't woven an elaborate tale, and I'd allowed myself to be carried away. I was starting to feel foolish for standing in the middle of the ruins, alone, silently waiting for a man who may never come, when I heard a twig snap.

It was the first sound I'd heard since arriving at the ruins, so I turned towards it quickly, vigilantly. The noise came from the small crop of trees where I'd been standing before moving into the courtyard. Even before the shape of a man appeared in the shadows, the hairs on my arms stood tall, and my body began to shiver. I knew I wasn't alone.

I stared at the spot where he would appear in only a matter of seconds with a hazy kind of focus, my eyes straining so hard that my vision began to go blurry. Then, I saw him, slinking from between the trees like a snake, seeking destruction.

It took me several seconds to recognize that his shoulders were too narrow, his stature too short. To recognize that the bulky, blonde murderer I'd been expecting was nowhere in sight. The man before me was slim and short. His eyes were sunken in, nothing but circular black shadows in his face. His clothes hung from him like rotten vines from a tree. He was a ghoul. A skeleton man if ever I'd seen one. He sparked fear in me more than shock because hadn't I always known it was him? Somewhere deep inside the thought had wriggled like a worm in the mud, burying its head but there all the same. I was surprised, but not because it was him. But because it had taken me so long to realize it. My heart clenched in my chest, and I took a step forward to formally meet the man who had tried to kill me. Who had set my life on a course of death and mayhem.

I tipped my head in greeting. "Mr. Barlow."

16

"Rose Beckingham." He smiled as he said my name, moving towards me like a lion on the prowl. He looked like a demon walking the earth. His cheeks were hollow, his skin pale and ashen. He did not look like a man who belonged amongst the living.

"You attacked Mrs. Hutchins," I said flatly. It was not a question, but an accusation.

He shrugged his thin shoulders and tilted his head to the side. "I did not intend to."

The distance between us was getting smaller. He moved towards me so slowly I could almost convince myself he wasn't moving at all. But he was moving. Like all predators, Mr. Barlow had focused his attention on me, and he would not stop until he received what he so desperately sought, or I defeated him. I intended it to be the latter. So, I took a large step backwards.

"I know that, too. You thought Mrs. Hutchins was me," I said, trying to sound calm. "I'm surprised a killer as adept as you could make such a mistake."

"Even a skilled knife thrower will miss his mark now and again. Do anything often enough, and you increase your chances for failure. It comes with the territory."

It was obvious now that the quiet, diligent secretary was nothing more than a façade. Mr. Barlow sounded haughty now, confident. He was proud of himself and his work. In his role as assassin, he bowed to no one, and he alone had control. It was incredible looking at him now that I hadn't seen the madness lurking inside. Though, part of me believed I had.

From the moment I'd met Mr. Barlow, he had unsettled something inside of me. Being in his presence made me uneasy, and where I usually found a rapport with the employees of the upper class due to my own low beginnings, I had no such relationship with Mr. Barlow. And at no point had there been a desire to have such a relationship.

"And attacking women while out on their evening walks is something you've done often?" I asked. I'd always been warned not to intimidate a predator. To never look them in the eyes or engage their killer instincts. Yet, I wanted to anger Mr. Barlow. I wanted him to reveal the truth of himself to me. I didn't want to see the humble Mr. Barlow serving Mr. Hutchins or the arrogant devil playing with his food before he took a bite. I wanted to see the true monster within. I wanted to see the anger that had to exist there for him to have killed so many innocent people.

He smiled, his teeth dull and gray in the moonlight. "Not often, no. Occasionally my mission has required it, but usually my clients are men."

"Clients?" I asked, barely able to contain my disgust.

"It is nicer than the alternative, don't you think?" He continued moving towards me, and I knew I would have to navigate around the large pedestal holding the statue of Hanuman in order to keep a safe distance between us.

"They are your victims, not your clients," I said, angling my body around the front corner of the statue. My right foot brushed a stone from the pedestal and a chunk broke off and skittered across the grass.

Mr. Barlow wrinkled his nose and shook his head like he'd eaten something sour. "Victims are innocent."

Mr. Beckingham's face appeared in my mind. He had been harsh with me on several occasions, but always out of concern for the real Rose, his daughter. He worried she was a silly girl who would grow into a silly woman, and he wanted me to help steady her. When I gave in and gossiped with her or giggled during church, he would narrow his eyes at me as though it was my fault. But he was not a cruel man. Now that I knew Lord Ashton, Rose's uncle, I realized he reminded me of Mr. Beckingham. They were both stern and solemn, but underneath it all was fierce love, like precious gems hidden inside a rock. One would only need to crack the surface to find it.

"The Beckinghams were innocent," I spat, my fear slowly morphing into rage. I could feel the weight of the pistol in my pocket, and I fought the urge to pull it out. He would confess his crimes to me. He would confess what I already knew: Mr. Barlow threw the bomb eight months before.

His eyebrows lifted in surprise before he tilted his head to the side, eyes narrowed. "What an interesting way to refer to your parents."

I clenched my jaw. I'd let my cover story slip ever so slightly, but it wasn't enough for him to understand the depth of my deception. So, I stayed quiet, my eyes boring into his, daring him to tell me the truth.

Finally, he continued. "Mr. Beckingham was the target. The deaths of his wife and any servants with them in the car explosion were incidental."

His voice was cold and grating. I wanted to cover my ears and block out the sound. I didn't want to hear the most tragic day of my life watered down to nothing more than an assignment. But I had to listen. I had to bear witness. Because the Beckinghams were no longer alive to do so. For their sakes, I had to look their killer in the face and let him know he hadn't won.

"I was in the car."

Mr. Barlow wasn't surprised by this information, and I didn't expect him to be. News of my miraculous survival was spread throughout Simla, and the killer would have a particular interest in the case, I was sure. But I didn't say it to surprise him. I said it to remind him that I was a survivor. That he had tried to kill me once before and failed, and he could fail again.

"I know," he said. "Miraculous that you escaped."

"Miraculous," I repeated, taking another step backwards when the space between us became uncomfortably close.

"Listen," he said, pressing his palms together and pointing his fingers at me, eyes lowered in what could only be false humility. "I'm sure you are not too fond of me given the circumstances, but you were not my target. I had no desire to kill you then or now."

"Had?" I asked, raising an eyebrow at his use of the past tense.

His lips puckered and he nodded. "Yes, unfortunately, due to your investigation, I have to kill you. You really did not give me a choice. You were too close to discovering my identity, and there is more work to be done yet."

I decided not to tell him that I believed Lieutenant

Collins to be the murderer until Mr. Barlow himself had broken through the tree line. Part of me believed I would have suspected Mr. Barlow eventually, but another part of me wondered whether he wouldn't have slipped my notice. As much as I hated to admit it, he had left no trail. Aside from a few references to his short, gaunt appearance, there was nothing tying Mr. Barlow to the crimes. He was a skilled assassin.

"And by 'work to be done,' you mean 'people to murder,'" I said.

He nodded, and I fought down a rising tide of nausea.

"How do you choose your victims?"

"My *clients*," he said, placing special emphasis on his preferred word, "are given to me by the American."

"The American?" I asked.

Mr. Barlow tightened his lips. Clearly, he had no more to say in regards to the identity of his employer. Then, the letter I'd found on the body of the assassin in Tangier came to mind. *I've named your target in previous correspondence and will not repeat it here. Kill him and I will send the money and name of another minister. Unlike your counterpart in Simla, use discretion.*

"Are there other assassins working with you?" I asked.

His mouth turned up in a half-smirk, but still he said nothing.

"Because I met a man in Tangier," I continued coolly. "He carried a letter written by an unnamed man. It discussed a previously agreed upon 'target,' but went on to say that the man in Tangier should use more discretion. There was mention of a Simla counterpart who had been a bit of a disappointment."

His carefully arranged façade cracked. Mr. Barlow's

brow lowered in concentration or frustration, I couldn't tell which.

"Who was this man you met?"

I shrugged. "He was dead before I had the opportunity to ask him."

Here, finally, I shocked him. His face went slack, every muscle falling into disuse as he contemplated what I'd just said. After several long, slow blinks, he regained his composure, but if possible, his face looked even paler. "And how did the man die?"

"I chased him beneath the wheels of a wagon." This was an oversimplification if ever there had been one, but while talking to a man who had attempted to murder me and sought to do it again, I didn't think it was the time to be humble. I wanted him to fear me.

Mr. Barlow ran his tongue over his teeth. "I wouldn't have thought you capable, Miss Rose."

"Then you have underestimated me." I could feel both the knife and the gun pressing against my body as if eager for me to pull them out, but I wanted to wait. I did not want to show all of my cards at once.

He shrugged. "Perhaps, I have. Though, I believe you have underestimated me, as well."

I shook my head. "Not possible. I know who you are. I know what you've done. I know what you are capable of."

"I am easily overlooked," he said, taking a step towards me, his hands folded behind his back. His posture looked casual, but I knew it was purposeful. I could scarcely imagine how many different weapons Mr. Barlow had hidden on his person—where he could stash blades and guns inside his jacket and trousers. "As I am a small man, most think me to be weak. That is their downfall. General Hughes certainly did not anticipate my strength."

I had already suspected General Hughes' death to be a murder at the hands of the assassin, but hearing Mr. Barlow talk about him so casually still rattled me. Perhaps, I did underestimate him in some regards. Despite everything I knew about him, I still expected something human in him to shine through. So far, I had only been disappointed.

"If you seek to surprise me with this admission, you are too late," I said. "I have long suspected General Hughes was murdered by the same person who murdered the Beckinghams."

"But you did not suspect me?" Mr. Barlow asked, brows pulled together. There seemed to be delight written in his features, giving him a coloring that more closely resembled a living, breathing human. It was almost as if being a normal member of society was not enough for him. He only came fully to life when he was able to kill.

There was no sense in lying. "Not at all. Not yet, anyway. I believe I may have come to suspect you eventually."

"That is a surprise. Once you spoke with the worker at the *White Tiger Club*, I believed I may have been discovered. I planted a clue pointing to Major McKinley that no one aside from yourself was clever enough to find, but the description the girl gave did not match that of the red-haired Scot, so I knew you would no longer suspect him."

"How do you know any of this?" I asked. I had been alone in the room with Rashi, and she had not shared her story with the police.

He smiled. "Though I have been described as one, I am no phantom, Miss Rose. You should simply learn to keep your voice down when talking with the help. I was standing near an open kitchen window while you talked with the Hutchins' native servant. It is how I also knew you would find my hut in the woods."

A cold chill moved through my body. "You followed me into the woods?"

"Does that frighten you?" he asked. "That I could follow you without you noticing?"

I didn't want to say yes, but my throat was closed tight in fear, not allowing me to deny it.

He continued. "I also know you have my weapon hidden beneath your jacket."

I glanced down at my arm pinched tightly to my side before I could stop myself.

"It is a favorite weapon of mine, so I hope you will not be bothered when I take it back from you. Well, I suppose you won't be bothered by much of anything when I reclaim it," he said with a smile. "You may be thinking me smug, assuming I can beat you in a fight, but it is only because I am positive I will beat you. It is not smugness as much as a fact. I have trained with the world's greatest fighters. I have slit more throats with that knife than you could ever imagine. And more than that, I have killed men with my bare hands. Men much larger than myself. I am sorry to say that you will not be much of a challenge."

"So, you think I should give up and turn myself over for death?" I asked.

He shrugged. "It would make things simpler, but I do not expect you to go down easily. And what do I know? As you tell it, you killed an assassin in Tangier. How the daughter of a high-ranking official found the skills to accomplish that I do not know, but it may mean I should temper my confidence until the deed is done."

As Mr. Barlow was discussing his own confidence, mine was slowly dwindling away. He knew about the *kukri* and had followed me on several occasions without my knowledge. Mr. Barlow was more skilled than I was. However, he did not seem to know I also had a gun in my pocket. That would be a surprise I'd save for the final moments of our fight.

Mr. Barlow took a step towards me, and I moved further around the side of the statue, maintaining our distance. I wasn't yet ready to begin the altercation. "Why are you working as a secretary?"

He sighed. I could tell he was tiring of talking. Soon, I would not be able to distract him with conversation, but for the moment, I was holding his attention. "Though 'The American' apparently does not believe me to be very discrete, working as a secretary for the insufferable Mr. Hutchins has allowed me unfettered access to some of the highest-ranking British officials. I sit in the room with them, learning their schedules and their habits while they do not even pay me a second glance. I am like a bug crawling along the edge of the room, they do not even notice my presence."

"Tell me about this American," I said. "Who is he?"

Mr. Barlow didn't answer, and I knew I'd caught him in an accidental slip. He'd told me more than he ought.

"You've already said he's the man who tells you who to murder."

Again, he didn't respond, letting me know I had guessed correctly.

"If you are so confident I will be dead soon, there is no reason to keep quiet," I said, tilting my head to the side, taunting him. "Or, are you beginning to think me more capable?"

Mr. Barlow smiled. "Your intentions are as obvious as your lies. We both know you did not kill the assassin in Tangier. He may be dead, but not by your hands."

So much for Mr. Barlow being frightened of me. "Then you have even more reason to tell me the truth."

He stared at me for a moment and sighed. "I was hired a year ago by a man who I know only as 'The American.' He paid me a healthy sum and told me to plant myself in India. There were no instructions for how to proceed, only a list of names of men I was supposed to kill."

"You do not know why you were selected or why you are killing these men?"

"I know I receive my payments on time and in full," he said. "That is enough for me."

I felt sick. That someone could be so callous in regard to human life. That any payment could excuse slaying the innocent. "Are you in contact with any other assassins?"

"Occasionally," he said simply.

"Did you know the man in Tangier?"

"Only from a distance."

"And you've never met 'The American'?" I asked.

"This is a waste of time," Mr. Barlow said. "Why should I explain myself to someone who will be dead in a matter of minutes?"

"Because you are a proud man who enjoys bragging about your accomplishments," I said.

He thought about my answer for a second and then shrugged. "That is true. I have been quite adept at integrating myself into the society here. Even with no prior experience as a secretary, I gained a job with Mr. Hutchins, which made all of my more covert activities possible. With him, I have travelled the country and become close to people in positions of power without ever once bringing suspicion upon myself."

"Until I came along," I said.

He nodded in agreement. "Yes, until you. I tried to frighten you away the other night with that warning note I left on your bed. But I quickly realized that would not work, that you would keep digging until I silenced you in a more permanent way."

I did not comment on his admission that he had been the one to leave the threatening note. "Who is your next target?" I asked instead.

He drummed his fingers together in the air and shook his head, taking two large steps towards me. I stumbled backwards, surprised by the suddenness of his move forward, and reached out to steady myself on the side of the statue. The stone crumbled beneath my fingers, and I wondered the statue was still standing at all. With my arm extended to keep myself upright, the *kukri* slipped from beneath my cardigan and fell onto the ground. I moved to reach for it, but there was no time. Mr. Barlow was too close now. I took several more steps away from him, my heart fluttering in my chest.

Mr. Barlow smiled when he saw the blade, as if he was greeting an old friend. "I think the time for conversation has passed, Miss Rose. It is late, and I have a busy day of work tomorrow with Mr. Hutchins. Especially now that his mother has been attacked." Mr. Barlow's smile slipped away, and the mask of apathy I'd come to expect from him settled over his face. "Absolutely dreadful the way a woman these days can be attacked on her own property. It is shameful. I hope the monster is captured quickly."

He couldn't help but brag. He wanted me to see the seamless way he could switch between the two sides of himself. So few people were able to see him this way, and even when they did, most of them were not long for this world after they discovered his split personality. If I was not careful, I would be another name on Mr. Barlow's undoubtedly long list of victims.

He bent down to retrieve the blade, and I knew I didn't

have much more time. So, I slipped my hand into my pocket, grabbed Lieutenant Collins' gun, and leveled it at Mr. Barlow. With the blade firmly in his grasp, he stood up ready to brandish it, but pulled back at the sight of the pistol.

"You are full of tricks, aren't you?" he said, a hint of admiration in his voice.

"I will shoot you," I said, my voice shaky with fear and adrenaline. "I do not want to, but if you come near me, I will pull the trigger."

"You don't have it in you," he said, taking another step towards me.

I tightened my grip on the gun. "You wouldn't be the first."

He moved towards me again, and my finger hovered over the trigger. "We already discussed your lies. There is no need for it. I know you did not kill the man in Tangier."

"I was not thinking of him," I said. "There have been others you know nothing about."

He raised his eyebrows in surprise, a smirk pulling one side of his mouth up. "What an interesting life you lead, Miss Beckingham. It is a shame I have to kill you."

"This is your final warning," I said. "Allow me to escort you to the authorities where the law will decide your fate or die here by my hand. It is your choice."

He pulled his lips to the side in thought. Then, he held up a finger as if an idea had just popped into his head. "I choose the third option."

Mr. Barlow lifted the *kukri* above his head and leaned forward into a run, charging at me. I had only seconds to respond, but I didn't hesitate. I pointed the gun at his chest and pulled the trigger.

I braced myself for the recoil, for the loud crack that

would reverberate through the air, for the heat that would rush through my hand. But there was nothing.

Just an empty click. The gun was not loaded.

Mr. Barlow paused mid-run, a sickening smile spreading across his face. He was evil incarnate, a monster in human skin. Everything about him told me to run in the opposite direction, to flee. "Perhaps, you should load a weapon before attempting to use it. Unfortunately, that is a lesson you will not have the opportunity to learn from."

With that, he lunged towards me again, and I ducked and rolled to the left, away from the statue. By the time I was on my feet again, Mr. Barlow was slashing the knife in my direction again, and it was only by the thinnest margin that he did not take a chunk of my scalp with it. I yelped in surprise and propelled myself forward, flat into the grass.

Mr. Barlow had obviously been confident his previous swing would meet me, because when he missed, he staggered in the direction of the knife, and it took him a few precious seconds to regain his balance. Seconds that allowed me to rise to my feet and sprint across the grass.

The ground was slippery with moisture, which made sense considering the sun would be up in less than two hours, and that made it difficult to find traction. The grassy lawn of the ruins was vast, and I knew I would not beat Mr. Barlow in a foot race. He was considerably older than me, but he had proven himself quite agile. I could try for the trees in hope of some sort of cover, but even that was a risk. So, I determined in a matter of seconds that I was safest using the statue as a home base. I could keep it as a barrier between us, giving me time and space to anticipate his moves and respond. I ran around to the other side and then jostled back and forth from one foot to the other, ready for whatever Mr. Barlow would do next.

"You do not even have a weapon," he snarled from the other side of the statue. "I am not going to chase you around this statue until morning. I will sit here and wait for you to exhaust yourself if it comes to that. But at some point, you will have to leave, and when you do, there will be nowhere to hide."

I stayed quiet. Mr. Barlow had been right before. The time for conversation was over. Now, all of my energy had to go towards surviving. Towards outsmarting a man who seemed to have every advantage.

I moved closer to the statue. It seemed dangerous to stick so close to the stone deity, but it allowed me to use it more as a shield. If he swung at me, I could dive behind the statue to protect me. And if he tried to run towards me, I would have less distance to run if I stayed close to Hanuman.

"You are being childish," he said, clearly annoyed now. This had gone on longer than he'd expected.

I did feel a bit like a child, running around the trunk of a tree to escape my brother's hands seeking to make me "it" in a game of tag. Except, in this case, the hands were a knife, and if I became "it," I would bleed out on the grounds of an ancient stone temple.

My recollection was interrupted by a grunt as Mr. Barlow raised the blade and lunged around the side of the statue. I clung to the stone leg as I ran around the base. Chunks of rock shrapnel blew into the air from the force of the knife cutting into the stone, and I could feel the entire structure rocking. It was not stable, and I worried if Mr. Barlow did not kill me, Hanuman would fall and crush me.

Mr. Barlow changed directions, pivoting to the other side of the statue and swiping out at me again. This time the blade was headed directly towards my face, and I had to duck down and begin pedaling backwards, my feet slipping momentarily in the grass. Again, the pedestal Hanuman stood upon quaked from the raucous going on at his feet.

"You will not win," Mr. Barlow growled. "You are alone and unarmed. End this charade and keep your dignity."

I was about to tell him I would never surrender, but before I could find the words, a shout echoed through the air. I thought it was Mr. Barlow, but then I caught a glimpse of his face between Hanuman's feet, and his brow was creased in confusion, and he turned towards the direction of the trees. I followed his eyes and saw a shadow emerging from the forest.

For a moment, I worried it was an accomplice of Mr. Barlow's coming to assist him. He hadn't wanted to tell me if he had any accomplices or how many of the other assassins he knew, and perhaps that was why. Because if things went wrong, he had someone ready to jump in and reveal themselves.

But then, I saw blonde hair reflected in the moonlight, and the broad shoulders of Lieutenant Collins. He was jogging across the grass.

"Stay away from her," he thundered, pointing at Mr. Barlow.

Mr. Barlow looked between me and the Lieutenant, and I could tell he was beginning to worry. He had not been counting on taking two people on at once.

The problem now was that he could not run away. If he did, his cover would be blown. He would be forced into hiding, and his time as an assassin operating under the guidance of 'The American' would be over. If he wanted to maintain the life he had built for himself, he had to defeat us. It was his only choice.

Before the Lieutenant could reach us, Mr. Barlow raised the *kukri* and swung again. I felt the wind from the blade slicing through the air against my fingers, and pulled back, circling around the statue again. This time, I noticed one of Hanuman's feet begin to lift from the pedestal. One more good whack with the blade, and the entire deity was going to come down on top of me.

"Rose, run!" Lieutenant Collins shouted.

He was still a long distance away, far enough away that if I ran from the safety of Hanuman, Mr. Barlow could catch up to me and slice my throat the way he'd intended when he'd attacked Mrs. Hutchins. No, sticking close to the statue was my only option, but even that was not a very good one any longer. The stone deity had protected me as long as he could, and soon, he would come down.

That was when the idea struck.

Before I could second guess myself—because there was no time for it, anyway—I backed up and then ran at the statue with all of my strength, pushing on Hanuman's ankle. For a brief second, nothing happened. Mr. Barlow looked at me like I was a mad woman, and then lifted the knife to launch another attack. However, before he could bring the weapon down, there was a loud grating sound and then the earth began to tremble.

He froze, looking for the source of the noise, and even I wasn't sure where it was coming from, but then, the statue began to tip.

The pedestal was crumbling beneath its weight. The ancient stones could not take any more stress. They cracked and fractured until Hanuman was tipping forward, heading directly for Mr. Barlow.

The assassin let out a yelp, and tried to run to the right,

but it was too late. With a sickening crash, the stone deity landed on top of the murderer and then settled into the ground. Aside from the echoes of the collapse moving through the trees, everything was quiet.

17

I stumbled backwards, still anticipating Mr. Barlow to push the statue aside and come after me again, but of course he couldn't. The deity was four times the size of a normal man, and even if the stones were weathered, it made them no less heavy. The assassin was dead.

"Rose!" Lieutenant Collins ran to me, hooking his hand around my elbow and pulling me away from the scene. "Are you all right? Are you hurt?"

I shook my head. I wasn't exactly all right, but I seemed to be miraculously uninjured.

"What happened?" he asked.

I answered in as few words as possible. "He killed my family. He tried to kill me."

Either Lieutenant Collins required no further explanation or he thought I was too shocked to make sense, because he didn't ask any more of me. "I heard you leave the house and stayed awake waiting for your return, but after several minutes, I could not wait anymore. It was too dangerous to be out alone, so I got up to follow you, and that is when I noticed my gun was missing."

"How did you know I'd come here?" I asked, eyes still trained on the image of Hanuman lying face first in the grass.

"I didn't," he said. "Which is why I was so late in arriving. I wandered the trails for a few minutes until I began moving in this direction. Then, I heard the sound of the blade cutting into the stone, and I knew something terrible was going on. I came as fast as I could, but obviously not fast enough."

"He may have killed you, Lieutenant. I'm glad you arrived as late as you did."

Lieutenant Collins grabbed my face. "He could have killed *you*, Rose. Why did you come here alone?"

I shook my head. I didn't have an answer that would satisfy him, so it seemed best to not give one.

LIEUTENANT COLLINS WRAPPED an arm around my waist and escorted me back to the Hutchins' bungalow where everyone in the house was awakened and the authorities were sent for. Mrs. Hutchins, who the night before had been hardly able to make it up the stairs, came dashing into the sitting room as soon as she was informed of the news by Jalini.

"Where is Rose? Where is Mr. Barlow?"

"Barlow is dead," Lieutenant Collins said with a surprising amount of vehemence.

She gasped and claimed the seat next to me on the sofa. "Are you hurt? What could have come over Mr. Barlow?"

I told her the same story I would spend the rest of the night explaining to the authorities. Mr. Barlow was not a secretary. He was an international assassin stationed in

India to carry out the will of an evil and mysterious leader.

She shook her head. "I knew there was something untrustworthy about him. Never trust a man with such pale skin, that is what I always say. Did you ever notice that, Rose? The man looked like he belonged in a coffin. And I suppose, now, he will be in one."

"If there is anything left of him to bury," Lieutenant Collins said.

Mrs. Hutchins wrinkled her nose at the image.

When the authorities arrived, they ushered everyone out of the room except for me, the Hutchinses, and Lieutenant Collins. I spent the next hours until sunrise replaying the events that led to Mr. Barlow's death and repeating everything he had told me about his organization over and over again until I had every word memorized. No one wanted to believe it could be true. Least of all Arthur Hutchins.

"I knew Mr. Barlow for a year," he said, shaking his head. It was the first time I could remember ever seeing him truly distraught. Even when his mother had been slashed with a knife, he'd barely registered any emotion other than annoyance at the inconvenience of it all.

"You thought you knew him," I said. "He had everyone fooled."

"Except Rose," Lieutenant Collins said, winking at me.

I'd decided not to tell the Lieutenant that he had been my main suspect until Mr. Barlow had appeared between the trees. It would distress him to think I'd thought so little of him. Anyway, the memory that I had been so badly fooled distressed me, as well. Though I had failed to notice Mr. Barlow following me around the city, at least I had not placed my absolute trust in him. If Lieutenant Collins had been the killer, I would have had to give up any hope of future investigative work. His betrayal would have ruined my faith in myself forever.

"And you say you believe he is the man who threw the explosive in the Simla marketplace?" a dark-haired Indian officer asked, his eyebrows raised in disbelief.

"I do not believe. I know it for a fact," I said.

"He may have attacked you," one of the officers said—a young blonde man with a pointy nose he liked to keep high in the air. He tucked a pencil and small pad of paper away in his uniform pocket, before continuing, "But we have no proof he killed your parents."

"He admitted it to me. Is that not proof enough? An eyewitness account?"

The man shrugged. "You were also an eyewitness to the bombing, yet you could not give a description of the man who threw the bomb. As certain as you may be that he is the culprit, we have to operate based on fact. And the facts are that we have no proof, and a man has already been executed for that crime. There is no reason to believe the investigation already carried out came to the wrong conclusion."

"I am that reason," I argued. "Mr. Barlow confessed his crimes to me in full. Ask Mr. Hutchins. I'm sure he will tell you he, his mother, and Mr. Barlow were in Simla eight months ago. I'm sure the timeline will match up."

Mr. Hutchins shifted in his seat. "I would have to check my calendars. I can't be positive we were here."

"Of course, we were here," Mrs. Hutchins barked, narrowing her eyes at her son. "How could anyone forget hearing the news of the explosion? It was dreadful. Absolutely dreadful."

The officers looked at one another, and I thought I saw one of them roll their eyes.

"And what of the murder of General Hughes?" I asked

with thinly veiled anger. "Will you say you have no proof of that, either?"

The officer's face turned a shameful shade of red, and I knew what his answer would be. Poor Elizabeth Hughes would always be viewed as a woman insane with grief for believing the truth about her father's death, and there was nothing I could do to change that.

"You will carry on letting his family believe he killed himself, then?" I challenged. "You will let them suffer when it is just as possible his life was stolen from him?"

"I think we would all be better served focusing on the matter at hand," the blonde officer said.

I stood up, every muscle in my body aching with exhaustion, and crossed my arms. "The people of this area would be better served if the authorities cared more about protecting them than covering their own botched investigations."

"Rose," Mr. Hutchins warned, his tone scandalized. "These men are here to protect us and—"

"Yet, Mrs. Hutchins was attacked on a walk last evening, and I was attacked several hours later. Yet, an innocent man was hanged in a public building and my mother and father were murdered in the marketplace. If they are here to protect us, then I beg they begin to do so. Until then, I'd like to ask them to show themselves out." My chest heaved with the force of my words, and though I could see Mr. Hutchins trying to catch the eyes of the officers to apologize, no one made a move to amend my words.

"I can show you gentlemen out," Lieutenant Collins said, before quickly adding, "If you have no more questions, that is."

The Indian officer shook his head immediately, but the

blonde hesitated, leveling a hard gaze at me. Finally, he too relented. "No more questions."

They were shown from the room, and I relaxed back into the sofa.

"That was inexcusable," Mr. Hutchins said. "Absolutely disgraceful. I'll have to send a letter of apology right away."

"Please, get to it," I said, no longer trying to be polite.

Mrs. Hutchins chuckled next to me, and feeling himself outnumbered, Mr. Hutchins stole away to hide in his office. I could imagine him writing a lengthy letter of apology at his desk, and the thought brought me only the smallest amount of joy. Though, it was overwhelmed by waves of helplessness.

"What will you do now?" Lieutenant Collins asked.

I hadn't realized he'd reentered the room, and I looked up at him, offering a measly smile. The truth was, I had no idea what I would do next. I'd hoped a confession from Mr. Barlow would be enough to secure the trust of the local authorities, but it was clear that was not the case. Once again, I was on my own, and the danger seemed to be mounting on all sides.

I sighed and pushed myself to standing. "For now, I think I will go to sleep."

"That is a good idea," Mrs. Hutchins said. "We all need to rest."

Lieutenant Collins stood and bowed as I left the room. Then, he called after me. "I would be glad to remain here throughout the night if you still wish it?"

I turned around and nodded. "That would be lovely, Lieutenant. Everyone would feel safer with your presence, I'm sure."

He crossed the room and grabbed my hand. His thin mustache twitched as he smiled. "I'm glad to hear that, though I think you know the only person here I care about is you."

It was the closest he had come to admitting his feelings for me, and I was completely unprepared to respond. Thankfully, he seemed to understand I was in no position to confess my feelings in either direction, so he bowed again, brought the back of my hand to his lips, and disappeared down the hallway in the direction of the guest room. I watched him go until I worried I would collapse on the spot. Then, I mounted the stairs, went into my room, and climbed immediately into bed.

After receiving an adequate amount of sleep, I finally had the energy to worry that my outburst the night before towards both the officers and Mr. Hutchins would leave me homeless. However, when I went downstairs for a very late breakfast the next morning, aside from some coldness from where Mr. Hutchins sat at the far end of the table, which I hardly minded at all, everything seemed perfectly normal. Mrs. Hutchins insisted the servants serve me and her double portions of everything so we could "regain our strength," and she declared I would always be welcome in their home.

"I know I was only attacked because of my resemblance to you, Rose, but isn't that even more reason for you to stay?" she asked. "It is not your fault the crazed man wanted you dead, and we are already alike enough to be relatives, so it only makes sense to me that we would adopt you as one of our own."

Mr. Hutchins grumbled into his coffee, but no one paid him any mind. I thanked Mrs. Hutchins for her kind words and promised I thought of her as family already. And in some ways—particularly the aggravating ones—I did feel a kind of familial kinship with the Hutchinses.

"Do you think you'll stay long in India?" Lieutenant Collins asked, trying to sound curious in a disinterested manner, though it was obvious he cared a great deal what my answer would be. "You came here for closure, and now you have it, don't you?"

Did I? If so, closure did not feel the way I'd expected it to. On one hand, I'd made all the connections I'd hoped to —between the man who had died in Tangier and Mr. Barlow, between the assassins and the Beckingham bombing, and even between the bombing and General Hughes' death—yet, I did not feel satisfied. The authorities did not respect my findings, and there was no telling how many more assassins lurked nearby. Plus, I now needed to uncover the identity of "The American." If anything, I had more questions than I started with.

"I am not sure," I said. "Time will tell, I suppose."

This answer did not seem to please the Lieutenant, but it did not devastate him, either.

At the end of our breakfast, I walked Lieutenant Collins to the door. "Thank you for staying the night and spending so much of your morning here. I'm sure you had better things planned for your day."

He grabbed my hand. "Better than stopping a murderous madman? I'm flattered you think my life could be so exciting."

I smiled to myself. Perhaps, the Lieutenant wouldn't have been so distraught if I'd admitted I believed him to be the killer for a few hours. That would certainly be some excitement.

"I do not mean to pressure you," he continued, his smile turning down at the corners, his brow fraught. "Especially after all you have been through these last few days, but I do hope you know how much I hope you will stay here in India."

"It is nice to know I have so many friends here," I said simply and noncommittally.

His lips pursed together like he was trying to stop himself from saying something else, and after a few seconds, he once again smiled and nodded. "You most certainly have good friends here who would all be sad to see you go. Myself included."

"Thank you, Lieutenant," I said, patting him on the shoulder. Then, I moved around him and opened the door. "But you must get on with your day. I will feel horribly if you waste another minute inside this house."

He moved towards the door and paused on the porch, turning around. "You are not planning to leave suddenly, are you? You'll give me warning to say goodbye?"

"I do not know that I'm leaving at all." I smiled.

Lieutenant Collins looked unconvinced, but he tipped his hat and then set out on foot down the long walk stretching from the bungalow and disappearing into the trees.

The door was halfway shut, and I was about to head back into the dining room, when I heard Arthur Hutchins and his mother engaging in an argument about hiring a new secretary. A deep exhaustion settled into my bones. It was less physical and more mental. I did not think I could sit at the table with them for another minute, so I quietly slipped through the crack in the door, carefully let the door latch settle into place, and then moved down the steps and towards the left, heading down the walking trail that ran the edge of the property. The same one Mrs. Hutchins had been walking down the day before when she'd been attacked.

I would need to tell Lord and Lady Ashton of what had transpired in India soon enough. It would be a difficult letter to write, and would probably require many back and forth correspondences to do the full story any justice, but they deserved to know the truth about their family's deaths, even if the police refused to see it as truth. It was a bittersweet kind of justice. I knew Mr. Barlow had been present that day in Simla. I knew he had been the one to throw the explosive device that had killed everyone inside our car, save for me. When I thought back on that day, on the thin man in rags moving towards the car, I could see Mr. Barlow's face now. It was discolored with paint and hidden in shadow, but I could see the wide, sunken orbs of his eyes, the gray glimmer of his teeth when he grimaced as he lifted his arm to throw the bomb. I could see him perfectly. I didn't know whether my brain had imposed his face over the memory or whether it had been locked away in my mind the whole time, but it hardly mattered. I knew the truth, and everyone else deserved to, as well.

Bird song echoed through the trees, and a warm southern wind moved down the path and lifted the hem of my pleated skirt. I pulled my jacket tighter around my chest. After everything I'd been through in the preceding days, being out alone in the shade of the trees should have frightened me, but it didn't. Yet again, I had found myself in a life and death situation, and I had come out on the side of life. I had killed the man who had sought to kill me, and perhaps I was being naïve, but I didn't believe anyone else would appear between the trees so soon.

Though, they would. In time.

Word of Mr. Barlow's death would spread throughout his assassin network. The news would reach the mysterious American, and sooner or later, my name would begin to circulate, as well. The leader would learn that I had been present at the deaths of two assassins they had hired, and my name would make it onto one of those lists. Just as Mr. Beckingham's name had. Just as General Hughes' had.

I needed to learn the identity of "The American." It was the only way to stop the assassin ring. I could continue to kill assassins as they came for me one by one, but it would be like cutting off the head of a hydra. Two more would appear in its place before the first could hit the ground. It would be like fighting a mythical beast.

I needed to understand what motivated "The American." Why did they choose the targets they chose? Why did they hire assassins the world over to take them out? If I could uncover the motivations, I would be closer to uncovering their identity.

As I walked along the path, I came to a fork in the road, a split where one path led around to the back garden of the house and the other led further into the trees. I hesitated for a moment before going right into the trees and further from the Hutchins' bungalow. A short while after making the decision, the trees opened to reveal a swath of blue sky. I moved towards the opening and found myself standing on a small ledge overlooking a steep drop. Rocks skittered out from beneath my feet and tumbled over the edge, rattling down the side of the cliff.

For the first time in several days, I wondered about Achilles Prideaux. Would he hear of my adventures in India? Would he hear word of the assassin I had killed? More than anything, I wanted to write to him and ask if he'd had any luck in convincing the British authorities to take the international assassin ring seriously. Because if he had also failed to find anyone willing to listen, then I was in trouble. In more ways than one, I was a few steps from death. One wrong turn, one mistake, and I could end up like General Hughes or the Beckinghams or any of the countless men and women who had lost their lives at the hands of these killers.

I toed a rock on the ground and rolled it beneath my foot before kicking it over the edge, watching it soar through the air before crashing onto a ledge below. Then, I turned and headed back towards the bungalow. I had letters to write and decisions to make, none of which would be easy. In my short time in India, I had accomplished a great deal, and, I feared, made myself a powerful enemy. From that moment on, I would need to look over my shoulder and be ever vigilant for my life could be in grave danger.

∼

*Continue following the mysterious adventures of Rose Beckingham in
"A Sudden Passing."*

ABOUT THE AUTHOR

Blythe Baker is a thirty-something bottle redhead from the South Central part of the country. When she's not slinging words and creating new worlds and characters, she's acting as chauffeur to her children and head groomer to her household of beloved pets.

Blythe enjoys long walks with her dog on sweaty days, grubbing in her flower garden, cooking, and ruthlessly de-cluttering her overcrowded home. She also likes binge-watching mystery shows on TV and burying herself in books about murder.

To learn more about Blythe, visit her website and sign up for her newsletter at www.blythebaker.com

Made in the USA
Las Vegas, NV
01 June 2024

90612280R00111